Eternal Child
Chapter 1

Thud! Clunk! Clang! Exiled; that's what those sounds meant. He would have slumped against the door and slid down to the ground in defeat if it hadn't been for the sharp and rusted spikes which dotted its surface. Instead, he staggered a few feet, clutching his ragged bundle of belongings tightly, and sat heavily at the foot of a kasha tree; its pale yellow leaves pulsing with the light absorbed from Orokuvar's two suns.

Looking back, he supposed he should have realised that this would happen but, for the first 12 years of his life, there had been no clues. He had looked just like every other citizen of Caamond. His skin had been luminescent with a smattering of crescent moon and star shaped freckles across his cheek bones; his face sweetly rounded and framed with an unruly mop of pale grey curls. His body had been lithe which hid the true strength it was capable of. The only thing that had made him in any way different to the rest of the Eternal Children was his eyes which had shocked but delighted his Founder so many years ago.

His beginning was like every other Eternal Child's. Eternal Children aren't born but are Found during the once yearly Silver Lunar Eclipse. As the silvery moon frees itself from Orokuvar's shadow, its sparkling rays of light, reflected from the two suns, fall on the Newlings, causing the crystals hung around their necks to sparkle. For the first 12 years of their lives, from Newling to Eternal Child, they are nurtured, guided and protected by their Founder.

Lunamor's Founder, Kuu, had found him in this exact way 12 years and 14 moon phases ago. Kuu had told the tale to Lunamor, often, as they sat by the flames of the fire on cold evenings, Lunamor's eyes growing wide with awe and wonder at the tale his Founder told no matter how many times he listened to it. Kuu always began his narrative with the fact that he nearly didn't bother to leave the city walls of Caamond on that year's Silver Eclipse

I had almost given up hope of ever finding a Newling the year I found you, Lunamor, but fortunately my crystal persuaded me otherwise. You are familiar with my crystal, which is an Aura Quartz; in some lights purple and in others green. It isn't the largest crystal within the city and had never predicted any great event before but, on the day of your Finding, it showed me that something momentous was going to happen. Earlier that evening, I had collected fresh water from the well in the centre of the city so that I could complete a short and fairly common ritual of prediction. The water is drawn from a deep, underground river which flows from south to north beneath the city. It is the city's only source of water within the city walls. As the hour of the Silver Eclipse approached, I used my pocket knife to shave a few wafer thin shards of my crystal into the water. Then, stirring it with a branch of the Kasha tree, I gazed into the depths to see what my crystal would tell me. Suddenly, the sharp splinters of purple and green began to spin faster and faster until a miniature tornado had formed in the centre of the liquid and began to rise from the wooden bowl it had been contained within. As it rose above my head, the water abruptly disappeared and the fragments of crystal formed to make a star which hung suspended above my head. I knew, instantly, that this was a good sign because, as you are well aware, Lunamor, stars are symbols of luck for our people. I immediately made my preparations.

That night, as the eclipse was almost complete, and as every ray of silver light was blocked by the body of our world, I left the city walls, along with three other hopeful Eternal Children, to attempt to find a Newling. As the heavy city gates slammed shut behind me, I set off in an easterly direction whilst my fellow Children took the other three compass points. Holding only a blazing Fire Crystal to light my way, I tripped over the shadowy and uneven ground and lost my footing, sliding down a steep sided hill and losing all sight of the city walls. At this moment, I was more scared than I have ever been in my 12 years and 456 moons. As you know, Lunamor, Eternal Children never leave the city walls, to do so is to invite certain death, but to ensure the survival of the Eternal Children Newlings must be found.

I scrabbled across the ocean of blackness around me, groping around for the Fire Crystal. The light of the Fire Crystal had been extinguished the moment it left my hand and, as I searched in vain for it, the first ghostly rays of the Silver Eclipse began to appear. It is a breathtaking sight and one that cannot be fully appreciated from behind the city walls. The silver rays begin to make contact with the ground, searching backwards and forwards, and then move on when their light reveals nothing. I was certain then, and I'm even more sure now, that if the light of my Fire Crystal had not gone out, I would never have found you. As it was, just as I got to my feet and brushed myself down, a million rays of lilac light shot into the sky and then, just as quickly, were gone. I began to walk, and then run, towards where I had seen the lights emanate from. I waited for that moment when the searchlight of the moon's sparkling rays returned to what its initial search had found and, therefore, allowed me to pinpoint the exact location you were to be found. The rays returned quicker than I would have expected. Almost as though the moon knew that it had found something special. As the moon's shimmering rays landed on you again, a solid lilac beam of light rose up into the sky and led me directly to you.

I've heard many Foundings being retold and never once, and never since, has there been a lilac ray; every other colour imaginable: teal, mauve, magenta, ocre, cyan but never lilac. As I reached the tiny bundle, and dropped heavily to my knees, the lilac ray began to fade away. My hands shook as I slowly uncurled my fingers and reached out to pull back one edge of the blanket. What I found there took my breath away and, as I struggled to take enough air into my lungs, your eyes locked onto mine. Eyes that were almond shaped and framed with thick silver lashes, as all Eternal Children's eyes are. Eyes that seemed to know me, know the world, know everything that has passed and everything that is to come. Eyes that were lilac and flecked with tiny shards of silver like Lollingite. Eyes the like of which I had never seen before.

It is as I tenderly scooped you up from the ground and held you for the first time, that I finally took note of the crystal hanging from a fine silk thread around your neck. All Newlings are Found with a crystal although the scholars are not in agreement about the reasons why. For thousands of moon phases, the most advanced Moonologists, the most accomplished Crystal readers and the wisest Ancient Studies elders have argued over the true purpose of those crystals. The one thing that they have all agreed upon, is the fact that the size and power of an Eternal Child's crystal is extremely important. Our history books show us that those Newlings found with the most unique and exceptional crystals have gone on to do great things. What I knew, as I crouched in the darkness, was that no Newling had ever been found with a lilac crystal. As I carried you back to the safety of the city walls that night, I couldn't wait to show you to those who might know what type of fortune you were going to bring.

Chapter 2

Whilst Lunamor had been lost deep in thoughts of his beginning, the two suns had met at the peak of their height. Their powerful rays now fought through the huge and tightly packed leaves of the kasha tree and caused his pale skin to glow radiantly. He knew that he needed to move. He knew that he couldn't just sit there and hope the city gates would open again to admit him entrance to Caamond, the place which had been his home his whole life. He knew that once a decision was made by the Perpetuates it was never reversed.

They had arrived at his small hut, where he had been living alone for the last 14 moons, as the first of the two suns broke over the horizon. They hadn't knocked or called out to warn him but had entered his home in a manner which showed they knew they had every right to walk in without permission. *They* were the Perpetuates. They were a group of five Eternal Children whose age was unknown. To the rest of the citizens of Caamond, it was as though the Perpetuates had always been there and there was no mention, in any of the Eternal Children's texts, that there had been any other Perpetuates before these five. They possessed superior knowledge in the three studies of the Eternal Children (Moonology, Crystal Reading and Ancient Studies) and no other came close to hoping to know as much as was known by these exceptional beings. The Perpetuates were also the owners of the largest crystals to be found within the walls of Caamond. It was they who had the authority, according to writings of old, to make decisions regarding the city. They ensured ancient laws were adhered to and also presided over the ancient rituals and ceremonies which took place throughout the year. In all matters, the Perpetuates' word was final.

The Perpetuate who had stood at the head of the group in front of him this morning was Opalua. Opalua's appearance was the same as every other Eternal Child but his importance was made clear by the flowing robes of golden silk he wore. These covered him from head to toe and fanned out behind him in a long, flowing golden river of material. The silken robes were ruffled at the neck and made it appear as though Opalua's head was nestled in a golden nest. He wore his grey curls long and had gathered some of them in a golden thread at the nape of his neck. Atop his head, sat a hat of great height which only added to his imposing presence. The Perpetuate's eyes were a dark shade of green and were speckled with tiny specks of red. When all was well the green shade would dominate but, if unhappy, the sparks of red would blaze as though on fire.

It was Opalua who had performed the ancient ritual when Lunamor had turned 12 years of age. Even now, 14 moons later, Lunamor could remember the powerful words of the ritual and the solemn gaze of Kuu as he had observed the ritual taking place.

12 year ago you had been found,
And now from Kuu you are unbound.
Make your way upon this earth,
Be sure to go and prove your worth.

Use the powers bestowed by stone,
To learn what yet is still unknown.

As the ancient verse had been recited, Opalua had taken Lunamor's lilac crystal in his hands and touched it gently first to Lunamor's left hand and then his right. To his left eyelid and then his right and finally he had pressed the unique crystal to Lunamor's forehead. This had signalled the end of Kuu's role as Lunamor's Founder and signified Lunamor's new status as an independent Eternal Child.

But this morning, the hopes and dreams he had had for the future had disappeared in an instant with the words Opalua had spoken. "Lunamor, you must leave the city and you must leave now. You are no longer, and never have been, one of us. Your place here in our city walls puts all of us in danger. We know not what you are, where you come from or what your purpose in our city may have been. For this reason, we cannot continue to allow you to live amongst us. You may take only a small bundle of clothing and your Fire Crystal. You will not be able to speak to anybody to say goodbye and you must never return. Child, I hope that you are able to find the place that you belong but it is not here, with us, amongst the Eternal Children." With that, three more Perpetuates had stepped forward and, with the four of them surrounding him, they had guided him swiftly through the city streets to the huge gate which barred the entrance to Caamond. To the side of the guard on duty stood the fifth and final Perpetuate. Even as Lunamor was being hustled along, he had time to notice the Perpetuate whisper something to the guard who flung the gates open. As Lunamor drew level with the guard he made eye contact, searching for hope, a way out, even a hint of sympathy but the guard's eyes remained cold as steel. Before Lunamor knew what was happening, he had been shoved outside and the gates had been locked tight behind him.

Lunamor shifted uncomfortably on the hard ground and considered his options. He could sit here and ultimately starve to death, he could bang on the doors and beg to be let back in or he could undertake a journey which no other Eternal Child had ever undertaken. He valued his life too much to waste it by sitting here and letting death take him. Calling on the sympathy of the Perpetuates and asking to be let back in was also not an option. As Opalua had said, even though he didn't want to admit it to himself, it was clear that he wasn't really an Eternal Child. This meant that his only option was to move on.

Eternal Children do not leave the city walls except during the Silver Eclipse and even then it is only the bravest of the Eternal Children who dare to enter the world outside their gates. Every Eternal Child was taught of the dangers outside the walls as part of their Ancient Studies but Lunamor had always questioned how it was known what was out there if no Eternal Child was ever said to have left Caamond. Tales were told of hideous beasts that soared the skies; hidden enemies that could not be seen with ordinary eyes; wild creatures who communicated in languages not known to the Eternal Children and evil powers beyond the capabilities of the people of the city. The young scholars were taught to appreciate the safety of their city and to respect the laws set out to protect them. And all thoughts of adventure, risk taking or thrill seeking were soon pushed out of the younger Eternal Children's minds with the horror stories of what would happen to them if they dared to show anything remotely approaching daring.

It had always struck Lunamor as odd that the ritual carried out at the age of 12 years, spoke of the Eternal Children making their way in the world and seeking out new knowledge. It appeared to Lunamor that what the Perpetuates really meant was for the Eternal Children to act as useful citizens of Caamond; to tend the animals, grow the crops, mend the buildings and heal the sick. The part of the ritual which spoke of learning what was yet unknown was even more unfathomable to Lunamor. What more could possibly be learnt within the confines of the city walls?

To question things that they had been taught was unknown in an Eternal Child. Lunamor's habit of trying to engage his peers in debate about the teachings of the elders and his barely masked cynicism made him stand out from the rest of the Eternal Children. He had first noticed, at the age of 12 years and 8 moons old, slight differences between himself and the other Eternal Children. For one thing, he didn't stop growing. Most Eternal Children were around 58 moonstones tall when they reached maturity (about 58 inches in human measurements) but now, at the age of 12 years and 14 moons Lunamor was 62 moonstones tall. Another noticeable difference was also in the shape of his body. His chest had begun to grow broader and he had developed visible muscles in his upper arms and legs. Eternal Children are extremely strong despite their slight frame but Lunamor's appearance visibly showed the strength he was capable of. Other Eternal Children had begun to look at him strangely as he passed. He would hear them muttering to each other when they thought he was out of hearing and it was clear, from the way they avoided his eyes, that he was a popular topic of conversation amongst his peers. Lunamor had taken to trying to slouch when he walked in order to disguise the fact that he was growing taller, he wore tunics that were looser and so hid the muscular arms and legs that were so unusual to the Eternal Children but he was unable to hide the most obvious difference between himself and everyone else.

As Lunamor had approached 12 years and 14 moons, a strange symbol, faint at first, had begun to appear on the left side of his neck. The first sign of the symbol was a silver sheen to the skin but, day by day, the silver sheen had taken on a more defined shape and had become a deeper grey/silver colour until it was now discernable for all to see. The symbol was shaped as a hendecagon with a small star at the top edge. Above the hendecagon, three small spheres formed an arc. Each of the vertices was joined by a straight line to the centre of the star. Lunamor knew that it was the appearance of this symbol, and the gossip of the Eternal Children, which had led to the Perpetuates' discovery of his differences and had ultimately led to his exile.

These differences meant that he could not possibly be an Eternal Child and therefore he did not need to continue to behave like one. Lunamor did not belong here but maybe he would find his place in the world, if only he went looking for it. This then, would be a voyage, a quest, an adventure and a journey of discovery.

Chapter 3

Decision made, Lunamor began to feel a little more hopeful that not all was lost. He still had his health and his strength. The position he now found himself in had also recharged that burning curiosity he had always struggled to keep hidden. He had always wanted to know what was really out there beyond the safety of the city walls. He just knew that the city he lived in could not be the extent of the whole world and he had never fully believed that everything that lay beyond the walls was evil. Now was his chance to find out. Curiosity was a trait which was frowned upon by the Eternal Children and was another thing that seemed to mark Lunamor as different. Kuu had taught him, early on, not to openly question what he was told. Even then, it seemed as though Kuu knew that Lunamor was not like everyone else and that, if this was discovered, it would end badly for them both.

Lunamor thought back to the last conversation he had had with Kuu which had taken place only the previous evening. Kuu had arrived at his hut, unexpectedly, just as the second sun set. As Lunamor had opened the door to the gentle tapping, he was surprised to see Kuu wearing his darkest robes of black and without his Fire Crystal to light his way. His Founder had pushed past Lunammor and into the house, quickly and firmly closing the door behind him as though he had not wanted to be seen.

"You need to sit down and listen to what I have to say," urged Kuu as he took a seat beside the low flames of the fire, "We really don't have a lot of time and they could come at any moment". Lunamor had stood for a few moments completely bewildered by Kuu's strange words and even stranger behaviour. Realising that Kuu was, in fact, scared, he took a seat opposite him and leant forward to take his hands. "What could possibly be the matter, Kuu?" asked Lunamor. Kuu squeezed Lunamor's hands gently before pulling his own hands away and placing them in his lap. He took a deep breath and began to speak.

"There is something I never told you about your Finding, Lunamor," whispered Kuu in a voice which betrayed his relief at finally being able to get this great weight, of a secret untold, off his chest. Kuu reached inside his robes and pulled out a circular slice of geode. It was large enough to almost fill both of his hands when held flat on his palms. The outer edge was gilded with silver and was slightly irregular in shape, with one side being almost flattened to a straight edge, so that the geode wasn't a perfect circle. The surface of the geode was highly polished and was made up of concentric circles: mauve, grey, silver and the exact same shade of lilac as Lunamor's crystal. As he held it out towards Lunamor, the flickering flames of the fire glinted off the outer edges and the mirrored surface of the geode and cast flickers of light across Kuu's face. Lunamor stared at the item in his Founder's hands. He looked up into Kuu's face and then back at the geode. With shaking hands, he reached out for the flat disk and took it from the outstretched palms. As soon as Lunamor's skin came into contact with the geode, he felt a strange tremor throughout his body and then a very strange feeling of oneness. It was as though a part of him had been missing and had now been returned. Lunamor felt as though this geode could provide him with the answers to all those questions he had kept to himself. Kuu took a deep breath and began to tell the tale of what had happened after Lunamor's Finding.

I knew as soon as I saw you that you were different. Despite the familiar freckles across your cheeks, despite the grey curls and despite the almond shaped eyes which looked into mine, the differences were stark. As I told you before Lunamor, no other Newling had ever been found with a lilac crystal and no other Newling had ever had the unique shade of lilac which was to be found in your eyes. I became aware of time slipping away and of the fact that I had been outside the city walls much longer than was safe. Scooping you up from the hollow in the ground in which you lay, I had intended to immediately make my way back to the safety of the city walls but a hard object, felt through the folds of the blanket, stopped me in my steps. I carefully reached into the blankets to locate the object I had just felt and pulled out the geode you now hold in your hands. I have kept this geode hidden all these years and have never breathed a word to anyone about its existence. Until today...

When I returned to the city that night I went straight to the Perpetuates. As you know, Lunamor, all Newlings must be announced so that their presence in the city can be recorded. I had unsettling feelings of foreboding about what would be said about the lilac crystal around your neck and the strange shade of your eyes and so I kept that geode hidden. I felt that the geode would be one difference too many and that you would be in danger if its existence was made known. The Perpetuates were as amazed as I by the sight of you. The Perpetuates locked themselves away from the rest of the Eternal Children for many moons and it was said they were consulting their crystals in the hope that they could predict what fate you were to bring to our city. They called on the keepers of the great books and demanded they be brought to them where they spent many more moons pouring over these books of old, searching for any mention of a crystal like yours but again their search appeared to be fruitless. With the passing of time, they emerged from their confinement and seemed to accept your place in our city as just one of many Eternal Children and I think I began to believe that they had actually forgotten about you.

Kuu leant forward with a fevered look in his eyes, "Until now," he gasped, "They know, Lunamor, that you are not like the rest of us. How could they fail to see that you are still growing and getting taller every day? How could they miss the muscles in your arms and legs which are becoming more noticeable despite the loose tunics you are wearing? And worst of all, how could they ignore the strange symbol which is most prominent on your neck? The Eternal Children are talking and their idle gossip has made its way to the ears of the Perpetuates. You are no longer safe here and I am sure the decision has already been made that they will have you exiled!"

As Kuu had been speaking, Lunamor had come to a horrifying realisation. He was going to have to leave his home. He was going to be thrown out into the strange and unpredictable world beyond the city walls and all because he was not the same as everyone else. The Perpetuates were willing to see Lunamor lose his life to ensure the safety of the rest of the Eternal Children. "What do I do?" beseeched Lunamor, "Where will I go?". Kuu gazed sadly at Lunamor and brushed away a lone silver tear which had escaped from the corner of one pale green eye, "You need to keep this geode hidden upon your person, Lunamor, and when the Perpetuates come for you, you need to make no mention of it. Do not fight them or try to beg to stay as you know they will not listen. I wish you well and will always hope that you are able to survive and that we may, one day, meet again". With that, Kuu had left Lunamor sitting beside his fireplace gazing into the depths of the geode on his lap.

Now, he held that same geode in his hands but he also held his own future. He had the freedom to make his own choices; to do what he wanted without answering to anyone else; to find out what he was capable of. It was just as he was having these thoughts, that he realised that the crystal hung around his neck was throbbing with a pale lilac light and vibrating against his skin. Compared to the other Eternal Children in his Crystal Studies lessons, Lunamor had always been a complete failure. His crystal had failed to ever show him what was to come and had never even shown the slightest flicker of life. But now it was pulsing with light. Placing the geode flat on the ground in front of him, he removed the lilac crystal from around his neck. Acting on instinct, he used his knife to shave a fine dusting of his crystal onto the surface of the geode, not wanting to waste too much in case this didn't work. He knelt down in front of the crystal and waited, with bated breath, to see what, if anything, would happen. All of a sudden, the sparkling powder began to spin and twirl, faster and faster, in the centre of the geode. Lunamor stared at it in amazement, holding his breath, and waiting to see what would happen next. Gradually, the crystal powder began to slow until it settled on the surface of the geode and formed the shape of a 6 pointed star. Oddly, one point of the star was much longer than the others and pointed south. Eternal Children have an intuition which is finely tuned to their crystal and it appeared that, on this occasion, Lunamor was no different. Instinctively, Lunamor knew what his crystal was telling him and knew that he needed to travel in the direction he was being shown. He replaced the crystal around his neck, tucked the geode back into the inner pocket of his tunic and took the first steps on what was surely to be a great adventure.

Chapter 4

With the suns high in the sky, Lunamor set off towards the south, leaving the city of Caamond behind him. Rolling hills of grass, broken by the occasional stream or scatterings of small rock formations, were all that could be seen in every direction. Lunamor, who had grown up within the crowded streets of Caamond and surrounded by the safety of the city walls, felt vulnerable and exposed. His alert gaze constantly roved over the distant horizon, on the lookout for any signs of danger. Unarmed and alone, he would stand no chance against the packs of moon hounds that were said to roam the grasslands around the city. These beasts were described as huge, at least 70 moon stones high, and almost the same size in width. Their fur was said to be a dark grey colour and often matted with the blood of their previous kills. It was told that their eyes were able to hold the light of the moon and, if one gazed into them, had the power to immobilise their prey in an instant. Their paralysed victims would not stand a chance. Lunamor felt a tremor of unease down his spine as he visualised these cruel predators. His imagination ran wild as he pictured them creeping up on him from all directions, their eyes searching out his in an attempt to make him their next meal.

By now, Lunamor had travelled a fair distance from the city and could only just make out the spire of the Perpetuates' meeting hall (the tallest building in Caamond) reaching up into the sky. He wondered if the Perpetuates had placed somebody in the tower to observe his progress across the grasslands. They would want to be sure that he had left and that he was not likely to return. He fought the temptation to raise his arm in defiance to wave at whoever may be watching. Instead, he continued on his way, making his stride appear more confident by straightening his back and moving on purposefully. He did not want to give the Perpetuates the satisfaction of watching him creep away from the city gates, cowed and rejected. Their last sight of him would be of Lunamor the adventurer; Lunamor, the first Eternal Child to actually fulfil the words of the ancient ritual by setting forth into the unmapped lands of Orokuvar to truly learn what is yet unknown.

Lunamor had been travelling for long enough to allow the two suns to travel a fair distance across the skies, only stopping to quench his thirst in the many streams he passed, when he began to see a dark, hazy shape on the horizon. It stretched from east to west as far as the eye could see and the closer Lunamor got, the more distinct the shape became. As he drew closer, he could see that he was approaching a vast forest.

The second of the 2 suns began its descent in the sky, in a slightly out of sync symmetry with the descent of the first sun as Lunamor reached the edge of the forest. Despite the fact that the grasslands were still fairly well lit, the depths of the forest were as dark as the night. No glimmer of light was able to fight its way through the densely packed trees. From his position at the outskirts of the forest, Lunamor could see taller trees, with black leaves as large as his head, which towered over the more familiar kasha tree. The trunks of the black-leafed trees were as large as some of the biggest huts in Caamond. These trees seemed to make up the bulk of the forest and were covered in a strange fruit, the likes of which Lunamor had never seen before. The fruit was pure white with veins of black running across it to give it a marbled effect. They hung, pendulously, from the branches in a teardrop shape. Some had fallen to the ground and split open, upon the bed of fallen spongy black leaves which had drifted down from the canopy, to reveal flesh which was also pure white.

Lunamor's mouth watered at the sight and he became aware of the gnawing hunger that had been slowly building up inside of him as he made his journey over the grasslands. He paused for a moment, to consider the folly of the choice he was about to make. He didn't know what these fruits were. He didn't know if they were safe to eat but, if he didn't eat, he would starve to death anyway. Decision made, Lunamor stepped into the shelter of the trees and reached up to pluck one of the fruits hanging close by. With his bare hands, he pulled the fruit apart, finding that it was surprisingly soft, and took a bite of the alabaster flesh inside. Lunamor moaned in delight, the flavours of the fruit filling his mouth; starting off sour and then almost unbearably sweet. Without conscious thought, Lunamor ate and ate until he finally realised that the deep ache within his stomach had gone.

It was only when he had finished eating, that he discerned a slight change in the quality of light coming from the open space of the grasslands behind him. The first of the two suns had already sunk below the edge of the world to the east and the second sun, to the west, was not far behind it. Before long, the silver moon would make its appearance and Lunamor would be forced to travel his way through the forest with only the light of his fire crystal to light the way. With his stomach now full, Lunamor decided that he should find shelter until morning. He felt a great weariness throughout his whole body. Apart from the ache in his legs, from the many miles he had walked, he was also more tired than he had ever been. He had spent the hours after Kuu's visit last night, pondering over his Founder's words and worrying about when the Perpetuates would come for him. Now, all he wanted to do was sleep.

Lunamor took his Fire Crystal from a pocket in his tunic and struck the blunt edge of his knife against the amber coloured stone. It instantly emitted a strong fiery glow, as bright as any that the moon worms emitted when they hovered over the inhabitants of Caamond during their breeding season. Hesitantly, Lunamor moved deeper into the forest. He found himself having to squeeze his body between the trunks of the many trees, they had grown so closely together. The branches above his head were so intertwined with each other that it was impossible to make out any light from above and so Lunamor lost all sense of time.

As he pushed his way, deeper and deeper, into the body of the forest, Lunamor held his Fire Crystal up high in front of him, looking for any place safe enough to take shelter for the night. With each step he took, his feet sank into the spongy leaves on the ground so that he almost bounced as he walked but this also meant he made little to no sound as he worked his way between the trees. Just then, Lunamor heard a noise which caused the hairs on the back of his neck to stand on end. Even though he had never heard this noise before he was still familiar with it. It was a sound that he had been taught to fear…

<u>Chapter 5</u>

The Eternal Children were a race who were fond of stories. Stories were shared at all social gatherings and celebrations, including at the coming of age rituals. These were often light hearted tales of the deeds of Eternal Children of the past. Of course, Eternal Children did not do brave and daring things, being a timid race, but their accomplishments in the arts of Moonology and Crystal Reading were legendary. The Eternal Children would tell stories of their ancestors; about long since passed Crystal Readers such as the one who had predicted the terrible drought and ensured the Perpetuates were able to avoid the deaths of many. They would share the legend of Marama, a Moonologist who possessed a unique ability to capture the power of the moon. During her time, as folklore told it, she had used her skills to guard Caamond against the threat of war and had kept away an army, which it had been predicted, was approaching their city. Thankfully that army never arrived and it was told that Marama had been able to use the moon's rays to create a forcefield around the city and therefore protect its inhabitants. This was a favourite story of the Perpetuates and was one which was illustrated upon the wall of their meeting hall.

Now, as the strange warbling howl sounded again, Lunamor was reminded of one of the more terrifying tales of the Eternal Children. He recalled the tale told to him, during the Silver Eclipse celebrations, by an older Eternal Child who was looking to terrify the younger ones who were gathered around him. They had huddled around one of the many campfires, under the light of the silver moon, and listened raptly to the tale that he told.

It was on the night of the Silver Eclipse, just like tonight, but many thousands of moons ago that the citizens of Caamond faced their greatest danger. Only two Eternal Children left the city walls that night in search of Newlings but only one ever returned. A few moments before the silver moon's rays were eclipsed, the two Eternal Children exited the city gates and went in their separate directions. As usual, the Eternal Children left behind clustered in the streets, eagerly awaiting the potential arrival of a Newling.

There is always a buzz of excitement at this time but also of unease. The Eternal Children fear for the safety of those who have gone in search of Newlings. On this night, they were right to feel this dread. It was just as the moon's silver rays had been completely smothered, that the most fearful noise was heard. It was a warbling howl which went on and on, as though the lungs of the beast which created it were so enormous that they would never run out of air. This was closely followed by another howl and then another. The Eternal Children within the city walls collectively held their breath. Suddenly, a scratching and scraping noise could be heard at the city gates. It was at that moment that the Perpetuate, Abalonwa, stepped forward.

Abalonwa faced the Eternal Children gathered before him and told them they had a decision to make. They could open the city gates and potentially allow in this strange beast which howled so terrifyingly or they could leave them tightly shut. This would mean the loss of life of the two Eternal Children who had left in search of Newlings. The Perpetuates have no misgivings about making decisions like this but often forced these difficult choices on the inhabitants of Caamond in order to make them appreciate the Perpetuates' judgements that little bit more. Just then, the silver rays of the moon began to make their reappearance and they highlighted the anxious faces of the Eternal Children standing before Abalonwa. The Eternal Children did not want this decision to be theirs, they didn't possess the courage required to be able to make that choice. Fortunately, the choice was made for them when they heard a voice coming from the other side of the gates. The Eternal Child pleaded to be let back in and so the bolt was drawn back and the terrified Eternal Child fell through the gates and into the waiting arms of those who were closest. The gates were hurriedly shut and locked tight.

It took a long time for the crowd who surrounded him to manage to get him to tell of what he had seen. When he finally spoke, they almost wished he hadn't. He told of a beast that flew so close over his head that he felt its claws tangle in his curls. It's wingspan was twice as large as the height of the city's gates but even that great wingspan was unable to lift its incredible bulk too far off the ground. Its body, arms and legs appeared to have the texture of leather and were the rusty colour of dried blood. Before he turned and ran, he just had time to see the repulsive creature swoop down to the ground and snatch at the Eternal Child beneath it. It then emitted the most terrifying howl, as though in celebration of having caught its prey, and half carried and half dragged its prize over the hills and out of sight. He hadn't waited around for the beast to return but had run, as fast as he was able, back to the city gates and back to the safety found within Caamond's walls.

For nights after that tale, Lunamor had struggled to sleep and Kuu had had to leave the lights burning low in order to get the young Lunamor to close his eyes. At that moment, as he cowered amongst the trees of the forest, Lunamor imagined the winged beast creeping up on him out of the darkness. The only thing that gave him comfort was the thought that it must have already found its meal for the night if the strident tones of its howl were anything to go by. He was also reassured by the fact that the trees grew so closely together that anything of any considerable size would struggle to make its way between the trees.

Feeling slightly braver, Lunamor continued his journey between the crowded trunks until he suddenly came to an area that was a small clearing in the forest. He spotted a tree directly in front of him of a type he had never seen before. Its girth was as large as his hut back home. The bark was the pale blue colour of a winter morning's sky and its trunk seemed to rise up forever. It was so tall that Lunamor was unable to see its giant, gold veined leaves way above his head. What had caught his eye though was the large hollow, just above his head, which was carved out of the huge trunk. The hollow was perfectly sized to allow him to climb into it and, if he padded it out with some of the spongy leaves from the ground, would make a perfect shelter for the night.

Relieved that he would finally get some rest, Lunamor strode over to the tree and, reaching up high, managed to hook his fingers into the edge of the hollow. Pulling with all his might, and pushing against the trunk of the tree with his toes, he was able to pull himself further up the tree towards the cleft in the trunk. Without warning, he suddenly felt sharp pin pricks piercing the backs of his hands and, with a cry of pain, he released his hold on the edge of the hollow. As he fell backwards, towards the ground, he saw two pale black orbs peering out at him from the darkness above. This was the last thing he saw as he hit his head and drifted into unconsciousness.

Chapter 6

The first thing he became aware of was the crackling sound of a roaring fire burning fiercely next to him. Then came the intense pain in his skull which caused him to reach for his head with both hands to check that it was still in one piece. Cautiously, opening one eye a tiny sliver, Lunamor glanced about but, other than the dancing flames, he couldn't see a thing. Still laying flat on his back, Lunamor opened both eyes and gazed up into the blackness above him. So little light came through that Lunamor assumed it must still be night. His head was resting on a soft cushion made of the spongy leaves which had been piled together in a small heap.

A sudden gasp made him turn his head to the right. "Ah, you're awake!" came a voice which was breathy like the sound of wind blowing through the leaves of a tree. "I apologise for biting you," whispered the voice again, "but you almost climbed right into my hollow on top of me! It was unfortunate that you also managed to bang your head when you fell. I've given you a dose of kasha root sap for the headache and I've treated the wounds on your hands". Although Lunamor could hear the voice, he couldn't see who it belonged to. The fierce flames of the fire blocked the owner of this odd utterance.

Lunamor pushed himself up onto his elbows and felt a wave of dizziness sweep over him. Almost falling back again, he took a few deep breaths, in and out, and then managed to force himself into a sitting position. At the side of him there was a fallen, moss covered log. Lunamor turned his body so that he was able to lean his back against its solid surface. Now, he was facing into the comforting glow of the campfire but was still unable to see who it was that had apparently bitten him and caused him to fall.

Strangely, Lunamor did not feel afraid. If he had been in any true danger the disembodied voice would have already done harm to him. Looking down at his hands, Lunamor noticed a line of miniscule scabs across each of his knuckles. They didn't hurt and were glistening with some kind of pearly ointment which had obviously sped up the healing process. The only damage to have been caused to him was the banging headache he was now suffering which was really his own fault for letting go of the hollow.

"I know you can speak because you were mumbling in your sleep," came the voice like a puff of air in the stillness of the night, "It's incredibly rude not to respond when spoken to!" The owner of the voice gave a disgruntled huff and then all was quiet apart from the gentle crackle and pop of the fragrant timbers of the fire. "I can't even see you!" said Lunamor, feeling slightly irritated at the tone of voice being used with him. Suddenly, there was a pattering sound as a handful of sand was thrown over the flames of the campfire. This didn't cause the fire to go out completely but dampened it down, just enough, so that Lunamor could now see who it was that had attacked him whilst he was looking for shelter.

Lunamor had never seen or heard of anything like what he was faced with as he peered through the curls and wisps of smoke from the fire. The creature, perched on a rounded rock, was almost insect-like. It had two sets of wings which were mint green in colour and almost translucent; they were threaded through with veins of a darker emerald green. "I'm Rendol," it declared and, as it spoke, its wings vibrated ever so slightly causing the glow from the fire to catch their glossy surfaces and bounce the light back at Lunamor. "I know *what* you are, I have heard of your kind before, but I do not know *who* you are," and with that the creature, Rendol, folded one of his pairs of arms and used the fingers of his other pair to tap impatiently on his knees.

Gazing in amazement into the face of the creature who had spoken, Lunamor noticed that Rendol's face was tinged a pale shade of green and was speckled with darker spots of a murky brown colour the exact shade of swamp water. His eyes were extremely large, in proportion to his face, and their black blankness reflected the image of the fire and Lunamor's own bewildered expression back at him. Lunamor also noticed that it had a row of teeth, top and bottom, which were needle thin and which explained the strange scars Lunamor now had on the backs of his hands. "How do you know of my people?" asked Lunamor, wondering how this strange creature could possibly recognise him when it was well known Eternal Children did not leave the confines of the city.

Rendol shifted himself into a more comfortable position on the rock and Lunamor noticed that his legs dangled several moon stones above the floor. If he were standing, Lunamor would have guessed the creature to be only 10 moon stones tall at the most. The creature clearly felt at home here and showed no fear of his surroundings so Lunamor tried to ignore the unease he felt. It was as though the dark depths of the forest were trying to close in upon him but the glow of the fire seemed to scare the shadows away. This caused a strange flickering effect so that Lunamor felt he could see movement out of the corners of his eyes. But, whenever he turned his head, he was able to see nothing but the densely packed forest and the darkness, like black cloth, which hung between each tree.

Dropping from the log, Rendol, his tiny body clothed in a mossy shade of green, came around the fire and looked deeply into Lunamor's eyes. "You have doubt in who you are," declared the creature in its breathless voice, "how can that be? Do you not know where you come from?" Lunamor wanted to move away. Rendol's gaze was searching and the piercing black intensity of his eyes seemed to mirror all of Lunamor's uncertainties. Passing through his mind were his doubts about why he was different, his questions about his beginning and most of all his need to know where he truly belonged. Shaking his head to clear it, Lunamor declared, "I.. I.. I don't know what you mean. My name is Lunamor and I have travelled from my home, Caamond".
"You have travelled through Caamond, you mean". Rendol said this as a statement, not a question and Lunamor was unsure how to respond. "That is not your home," said Rendol in his strange, breathy voice. "My people, the Skogners, have seen your ancestors, many thousands of moons ago, and they are like you in appearance, they do not come from this place you call Caamond".
"How can you know this?" asked Lunamor, the urgency for answers apparent in his voice, "Where are they now?"

"It is a strange tale to tell, Lunamor, and will not provide you with the enlightenment you seek. I am able to only tell you what has been passed down through generations of Skogners. I fear that, to tell you this story, will leave you with more questions than you already have," said Rendol in a gentle puff of breath.

"I have to know what you know of my people," demanded Lunamor, "I am exiled from Caamond and now belong nowhere". Lunamor described the ways in which he was different to those of his city and retold the words of the Perpetuates who had ordered him to leave. Rendol listened quietly, throughout Lunamor's recount, giving only the occasional quiver of his wings in annoyance or the odd huff of disgust at the unfair way in which Lunamor had been treated. When he had finished speaking, Rendol settled himself on the log beside Lunamor and, as sparks from the fire drifted lazily up towards the canopy of the trees, he began his tale.

My people are the Skogners. We are forest dwellers and, as such, we never leave the forest. The trees around us provide us with everything we need and so we have never had to make those journeys that some races feel are so essential. We have been in the forests of Morupo for so many moons that the stories of how we came to be here have been long forgotten but the myth which tells of the arrival of your people has been told for several thousands of moons and is still told today. It is only now that I realise that it is, in fact, not a myth but a story of true adventurers.

Beneath and within the trees of Morupo, it is not possible to know what is going on in the outside world. We are not able to see the skies above, we hardly know when it is day or night. The phases of the moon and the suns' journeys across the sky mean nothing to us here. For this reason, it is hard for us to know the time of year when they arrived.

Their arrival was witnessed by a young Skogner who kept herself hidden within the hollow of a tree, much like where you found me napping today. Who knows what would have happened if she had made herself known, but her fear of these unknown creatures kept her frozen in place within the trunk of the tree.

The story goes, that there were five of them, all tall like you. The young Skogner heard their approach, and, when she peeked out from her hiding place, she saw their arrival in the clearing in front of her. They had the same soft grey curls, freckles that exactly matched your own and the strange symbol, which you also possess, on their necks. They carried weapons; long spears with handles wrapped round with the black vines from the nott tree; bows and arrows carved from the pale blue wood of the kodu kayu tree and curved knives, as big as a Skogner, which they used to chop at the branches that blocked their path.

They sat down to rest in the circle formed by the trees around them and whilst enjoying a meal of dried fruits they took from their bags, they spoke to each other of their journey. It appeared that they were on a mission of some importance, based on a prediction handed down by their ancestors. They did not speak of this prediction, only to say that they had lost sight of the shower of stars they had been following, the minute they entered the forest of Morupo. They were concerned that, by the time they emerged from the forest, the stars would have gone and they would then be unable to complete the task they seemed to have been set. For this reason they decided not to rest any longer, and continued their journey through our woods. No other Skogner saw them, as they travelled through the depths of Morupo, and their likes were never seen again.

Rendol's story ended just as the embers of the fire were beginning to die out. Lunamor was exhausted and his tired mind struggled to make any sense of what Rendol had told him. He didn't know what to think about the fact that there were others out there like him, others who had made a journey similar to his, albeit in reverse. What he did know was that he didn't feel quite so alone. This little comfort, the warmth of the fire and the exertions of his day all combined to push him over the brink of consciousness and into a deep and dreamless sleep.

Chapter 7

Lunamor awoke suddenly, not really sure what had roused him. The fire had completely burnt itself out but, due to the thick canopy of the trees above, it was not possible for Lunamor to know the hour. There was a grey quality to the light which seemed to suggest that it was daytime but it was anybody's guess exactly what the time was. As Lunamor came more fully awake, he could just about make out the huddled back of Rendol who sat a short distance away. The Skogner seemed to be holding something in his hands but Lunamor was unable to make out what it was. More alert now, he reached for his Fire Crystal and brought the light to life with his blade.

As the crystal's warm glow filled the clearing, Lunamor could see more details of where he had spent the night. The clearing was the same one in which he had tried, unsuccessfully, to climb into the hollow. Rendol had sensibly built the fire next to him, rather than trying to move the Eternal Child, which would have been impossible given the difference in their sizes. The clearing was edged with more of the blue trunked trees which Rendol had called the koda kayu tree. Dotted in between, were the smaller fruit trees from which Lunamor had eased his hunger the day before. What Lunamor had not noticed was a small stream which wove its way through the centre of the clearing. His mouth feeling as dry as moon stone dust, Lunamor sat up, intending to quench his thirst with a drink of the refreshingly clear water which bubbled past. It was then that he noticed what Rendol was holding and it was then that he also realised what had woken him so abruptly.

In his tiny hands, Rendol held the precious geode which Lunamor had kept hidden in the inner pocket of his tunic. He was examining it closely, turning it this way and that to inspect the silver gilded edges. As Lunamor watched, Rendol was running one of his 14 fingers around the series of circles which rippled outwards towards the edge of the geode like the patterns made when a moon stone is dropped into a puddle. Lunamor lunged from the bed of spongy leaves where he had slept and snatched the geode out of Rendol's hand, knocking the Skogner over as he did so. "What do you think you are doing?" demanded Lunamor, infuriated, "That's mine and you had no right to take it from me while I was sleeping!".
"Apologies," puffed Rendol weakly, his voice now like the faintest breath of wind, "it had slipped from your tunic pocket as you slept and I was afraid that you might roll onto it and break it. Anyway, you should be taking better care of something so rare and precious". His anger forgotten, Lunamor looked at the Skogner questioningly. "You have seen something like this before? I need to know! Where and when?"

Rendol had managed to right himself and now hovered a short distance above the floor on wings which fluttered so quickly they were only a green blur. He had both sets of arms crossed and was clearly disgruntled at the way he had been pushed to the ground even if his fall *was* cushioned by the black leaves of the nott tree. Lunamor could see in the Skogner's face that he was considering not answering, just out of spite, but Rendol's love of talking soon induced him to make up his mind. "I have never seen a geode like this but I have heard of one described which matches this one perfectly. I never thought it actually existed and thought it was just a legend of my people but now we have the proof right here. I feel so honoured to have been able to hold it in my hands if only for a short time. You must be hungry and thirsty after your long sleep. Sit and refresh yourself and I will tell you the prophecy told to my people so long ago and which has now been shared as legacy for thousands of moons".

Lunamor used his cupped hands to take a long drink from the crystal clear water of the stream and then collected a few of the strange fruits of the nearby nott tree. He returned to his seat beside the cold ashes of the fire and leant his back against the fallen log. Rendol, seeing that Lunamor was now settled and ready for the story he had to tell, flittered for a few minutes, indecisive about where to sit, and then settled on the log beside Lunamor's head. In a voice which was as gentle as a sigh, Rendol retold the legend he had heard as a young Skogner.

Aeons ago, a lone traveller crossed through our lands and shared with us a tale we have never forgotten.

We had never seen one such as him before, for he called himself a Tugarl. He was an odd looking specimen, much taller than you but he walked with a stooped back. His skin was incredibly wrinkled and so thin you could almost see through to the bone underneath. Despite the heat of that day, he was wrapped around in furs taken from all kinds of animals, many of which we had never seen within our forests. But it was his face which drew attention the most. The eyes were like windows of wisdom. The moment our ancestors looked into their glassy surface, a strange thing happened. No word was spoken but, as he gazed back at the Skogner in front of him, the Tugarl seemed to absorb our history and make it his own. In that split second, he knew everything that we had taken thousands of moons to learn and he saw everything that we had ever seen.

He then held out a hand and placed it gently on the head of the Sknogner who had greeted him. No words were exchanged but, in that moment, the Skogner saw what it was the Tugarl wanted to share. This Tugarl had been given a very important mission, he was to carry a prophecy across our world to share with all he encountered. This is that prophecy.

Amidst a shower of stars it will descend,
Allowing the Crystal Bearer to transcend,
The danger our prophets do portend,
On him our freedom does depend.

Before the Tugarl removed his hand from where it rested he shared a vision of an object. The very object, in fact, which you hold in your hands this very moment. A geode of incredible beauty, rimmed with silver, its surface like polished glass, and displaying a spectrum of purple shades never seen anywhere else in our world.

As Rendol finished his breathy retelling, he flew into the air excitedly and hovered nose to nose with Lunamor. "The prophecy is real! The geode is real! That means the chosen one is also real! Do you know what this means, Lunamor? It means that you are the Crystal Bearer!"

Shakily, Lunamor gazed into the glossy veneer of the geode and his own reflection stared back at him. For the first time, he didn't recognise himself. His whole world had been shaken the moment he had been exiled. To discover he was not a true Eternal Child, and did not belong in Caamond, had been devastating enough but now he was faced with the knowledge that there may not be anyone out there like him. He may not ever find somewhere that he would fit in.

Chapter 8

Impatient to continue his journey, but unsure of the direction he should head in, Lunamor pared a few more splinters of crystal onto the geode and waited. Rendol looked on curiously, whilst hovering in the air at Lunamor's shoulder. As before, the sparkling shards began to spin and then settle into the same six sided star Lunamor had witnessed the first time. Rendol gasped in surprise. Turning to face the direction in which the longest point of the star indicated, Lunamor tucked the geode safely into the concealed pocket inside his tunic.

"Where are you going?" breathed Rendol, when it looked like Lunamor was going to walk off without another word. "How do you think you are going to navigate your way through this forest safely when you couldn't even survive the first night without running into trouble?" he asked, with a small smirk on his face.
"YOU were the trouble I ran into. If it hadn't been for you I would have been well on my way by now", said Lunamor.
"If you think I am the danger you need to be wary of then you Eternal Children really do know nothing," harrumphed Rendol huffily and turned away in a sulk.
"I may know nothing of the world outside the city walls of Caamond, but I am sure I have more chance of warding off an attack than you have," stated Lunamor hotly.

By now the Skogner's face was a deep shade of emerald green so great was his anger at the dismissal in Lunamor's tone. "You have no idea what dangers are out there! Not everything in the forest of Morupo can be beaten by sheer strength alone and you would do well to learn from those who are willing to teach you!". Instead of the gentle exhalations in which Rendol had spoken previously, this last was said in a stormy voice as though the fiercest winds were whipping around the windows of the tallest towers of Caamond. Lunamor took a step back in surprise, "Are you offering to be my guide through the forest?".

Having lived within the confines of Caamond all his life, and having been shielded from the harsh reality of the threats outside its city walls, Lunamor was unused to such expressions of bravery. Eternal Children did not put themselves in danger for anything other than searching for Newlings and here was a perfect stranger who was willing to put his life on the line in order that Lunamor could continue his journey. Feeling humbled, Lunamor added, "I would like it if you were willing to be my teacher and my guide". Rendol turned to face the traveller before him and, looking slightly calmer, nodded that he was willing to take on that role. "As long as you are aware that I can go no further than the edges of the forest," Rendol clarified, "We do not leave the boundaries of the forest for any reason". Lunamor reached over to take one of the Skogner's tiny hands in his own and gave it a gentle shake, a world wide gesture of reconciliation and friendship.

They began their trek through the forest with Lunamor setting the pace and Rendol fluttering at his shoulder. The Skogner kept up a steady stream of commentary on everything that they passed, pointing out strange flowers and trees the likes of which Lunamor had never seen before. One flower in particular excited Rendol as he showed Lunamor how to take the enormous teal coloured flower from its stem and then tip it up to drink the fragrant nectar found within it. Once its contents were drained, Rendol then showed Lunamor how to curl the petals into a thin tube. This was then stowed away in the small bundle Lunamor still carried on his back. Knowledgeably, Rendol assured the sheltered Eternal Child that when the petals dried out they could be added to boiling water and would make a delicious broth. He also explained that the flower's nectar provided energy and was able to sharpen the senses of anybody who ingested it. Even as Rendol finished explaining all of this, Lunamor could feel the nectar taking effect and he continued onwards with renewed vigour and heightened senses.

Rendol was able to find the easiest route through the trees and, gesturing with one of his four arms, indicated the paths they should take which would offer them the least resistance. This meant that they managed to cover a great distance in a short time and Lunamor was well aware that he would never have made it this far by himself. After they had been travelling for what felt like an eternity to Lunamor, a family of strom hogs ran across the trail in front of them, making both of them jump. "We should really hunt for something more filling for you to eat," declared Rendol as he watched the strom hogs disappear into the cover of the trees. "I can live on the fruits and the flowers of the forest but you will not get far on your journey if you do not eat something more substantial".
"I've never had to catch my food. All food in the city of Caamond is kept in the animal pens and is butchered by those Eternal Children who have taken that on as their vocation. I don't think I could kill an animal no matter how hungry I got".
"It really isn't as difficult as you imagine," reassured Rendol, "And one will find they can do anything when they are in need of sustenance".

Under the Skogner's tutelage, Lunamor was able to fashion a spear from a branch of the kasha tree. He used his knife to whittle the ends so that it formed a sharp point and then wrapped the toughened vines of the nott tree around the handle to give him a better grip. After that, Rendol showed Lunamor how to take the spongy black leaves of the nott tree and how to pound them into a black pulpy paste. This paste was then added to the end of the spear. Rendol assured Lunamor that, although the fruit of the nott tree was highly nutritious as well as being extremely tasty, the ebony leaves were incredibly poisonous. Lunamor was now armed with a weapon he could use to hunt but that he could also use to defend himself should the need arise.

Apprehensively, Lunamor hid his body behind the large trunk of the kodu kayu tree Rendol had suggested, whilst the Skogner zipped in and out of the trunks of the trees into the darkest parts of the forest. The plan was for Rendol to flush out any wild strom hogs that may be hiding there so that Lunamor could pounce and attack them with his spear. It wasn't too long before all was silent and Lunamor was completely alone. He shifted anxiously as the minutes ticked by, every little sound causing him to flinch. The heavy weight and tickle of a huge crystal spider crawling across the back of his neck almost caused Lunamor to abandon his hiding place but, with a shudder, he managed to shake it off and kick it into the underbrush. He watched in revulsion as it righted itself on spindly white legs, cloudy white skin stretched tightly across its fat little body, and dug its way into the layer of spongy leaves which coated the forest floor. Just when he had almost given up hope, and was starting to wonder if Rendol had abandoned him after all, Lunamor heard the crashing of branches and the heavy panting of something running towards him. He braced himself to attack and, as the strom hog raced past his hiding place, Lunamor struck it in the back of the neck with the jagged end of his spear. The spear was wrenched from Lunamor's grip as the strom hog's forward momentum carried it onwards another three or four paces and then it dropped to the floor as the poison from the nott tree leaves entered its blood stream and paralysed it. Whooping with excitement, Rendol burst from the trees in a flurry of green wings, "You got it! You got it!" he crowed.

They decided to make camp for the night and Lunamor used his Fire Crystal to get a cooking fire going. Together, he and Rendol had been able to strap the hog to a large branch which they strung across the fire, rotating it every so often. As the meat slowly roasted, filling the air with a delicious aroma, Lunamor and Rendol lay back on the spongy floor of the forest. "Where are your family Rendol?" asked Lunamor, watching the curls of smoke and stray sparks from the fire drift upwards. "Lost," was the answer he received. Thinking that the usually talkative Rendol was going to say no more, Lunamor's eyes began to drift closed but then the Skogner began to speak again.

The forest of Morupo is immensely wide. It stretches from east to west, almost reaching the boundaries of Orokuvar at either end. It acts as a significant barrier between the south and north of our realm, so much so that those from the north and those from the south very rarely meet. The inhabitants of Orokuvar don't journey through these forests without much preparation and courage. Even I don't know of everything that can be found within its boundaries.

Travellers through the forest are so rare that only once, in my lifetime, have I encountered an outsider. Other than you, that is Lunamor. On the day that I lost my family, we had been sharing our evening meal and getting ready to settle down in the tree hollows we had made our home. A larger hollow for my parents, one for my elder brother and then one for me. And then...I just don't know what happened. The trees seemed to almost part on their own. Even the mightiest trees swayed to one side and some of them were even snapped clean in half. I stared in horror at the chaos in front of me but I could see nothing that would account for the pandemonium going on in the clearing. The noise was terrible; the snapping of gigantic tree trunks as though they were nothing but splinters of wood; thundering booms as though giants were stomping across the clearing and a maelstrom of debris flying around in the air as though a tornado had arrived. But still, no visible sign of what was causing this.

From my hiding place, I watched as everything suddenly became still and quiet. I peeked over the edge of the hollow; it was as though the air shimmered and everything seemed to blur together in front of me. Before I knew what was happening, my parents and my brother were snatched, as though by an invisible hand, out of their shelters and the tremendous noise began again as whatever it was began its retreat back through the crowds of trees. That was the last I ever saw of them.

Whilst the poor Skogner spoke, Lunamor had listened, aghast, to the devastating tale he had to tell. Back in Caamond, he had heard similar myths of invisible giants who strode across the world snatching their prey. The fearful Eternal Children spoke of how nothing could stop these beasts as their victims couldn't even see them coming. Now, as a solitary tear dropped from the Skogner's huge black eyes, Lunamor reached out a hand to pat at his shoulder comfortingly.

Impatiently brushing his tears away with the cuff of one green sleeve, Rendol jumped up to attend to the hog roasting on the spit. The two ate a hearty meal of hog roast followed by more of the fruit from the nott tree and then they settled down for the night to sleep. Before long, the forest was filled with the gentle inhalations and exhalations of Lunamor and the repetitive puff, puff, puff as Rendol snored by his side.

Chapter 9

For many days, Lunamor and his talkative companion travelled through the forest without incident. Luckily for Lunamor, the forest of Morupo was narrower, north to south, than it was east to west and Rendol estimated that they should arrive at its border before too long. The crowding of the trees and the near constant darkness made Lunamor feel almost suffocated and he was eager to be out in the open again where he could look upon the suns and the silver moon. But neither he nor Rendol could have predicted what would happen when they reached the boundaries.

The day had started just like every other day Lunamor had spent in the forest with Rendol. The travellers had put out their campfire, eaten a hearty breakfast of koda kayu tree roots and then set out south. "I think we will make it to the edge of the forest today," stated Rendol with a happy sigh, "Can you see how the trees are thinning out?". Lunamor could not see this at all but took Rendol's word for it and so his step was made lighter with the hope that he would soon be free of the confines of the forest. Despite the fact he had spent so many days amongst the trees, he was still not comfortable with the way that the shadowy depths seemed to close in on him whenever he was not looking.

Rendol prattled on and on and Lunamor listened with only half his attention on what the Skogner was saying. His thoughts were consumed with what would greet him when he left Morupo. He would be on his own then as Rendol would be staying behind in the forest. What dangers would he face? Would he have the strength and the courage to confront them? Would he even make it to whatever destination his geode was guiding him to? Sometimes, the thought of the challenges in front of him became so great that he would imagine turning back. He could stay with Rendol in the forest. Or he could return to Caamond and tell them what little he had learnt. Who knew, they might welcome him back because of the knowledge he could bring them of what he had seen and heard.

All of a sudden, Lunamor felt Rendol's seven tiny fingers grip his shoulder tightly. He turned to brush the Skogner off in irritation but noticed the look of horror on Rendol's face. "What is it?" said Lunamor urgently, "What's wrong?". It was then that Lunamor became aware of an odd noise. It was a combination of whistling and buzzing and, although the noise didn't seem particularly threatening, it sent a trickle of fear down Lunamor's back. "Run!" gasped Rendol and he shot off through the air at a neck-breaking speed through the trees.

Lunamor raced after the surprisingly fast Skogner, ducking under low hanging branches and leaping over the uneven terrain of the forest floor. With a cry of pain, he felt the sharp lash of a slender tree branch slice across his cheek but he raced on. Over the pounding of the blood in his ears, Lunamor could hear the strange noise getting louder and louder and threw a quick glance over his shoulder as he ran. What he saw almost stopped him in his tracks in terror.

Swarming towards him were a dozen airborne insects. They were small, each one only as big as his hand, with thin, pointed bodies like a short arrow. Along the lengths of their bodies were three pairs of wings, the middle set punctured with a series of holes. It was these wings which appeared to be making the whistling noise that had warned Lunamor and Rendol of their approach. In the fleeting glimpse Lunamor had of them, he could not fail to notice the tips of their tails. Each tail was armed with a multitude of razor sharp barbs which, bundled together in a tight cluster, glinted and shone, mimicking one of the most precious crystals of all-the diamond.

"What are they?" panted Lunamor as he continued his reckless dash through the trees. Rendol, who seemed to be tiring and had slowed his pace a little,answered in short gasps, "They're olmflies. Extremely deadly. No cure for venom".
"Isn't there something we could do? I don't know, maybe try and knock them out of the air with the spear?" Lunamor wheezed. He didn't think he could continue running at this pace for much longer. "We would have no chance, they would surround us before we had even managed to hit one of them. Our only hope is to keep running and maybe reach the edge of the forest before they get to us. Olmflies won't fly out into the open," panted Rendol.

The whistling buzz seemed to be getting louder and louder. He didn't know if he was imagining it but he could almost hear the lethal barbs at the ends of their tails rubbing against each other and making a noise similar to that of a knife being sharpened. Fear spurring him on, Lunamor ran faster than he had ever run before.

Suddenly, Rendol gave a cry of relief, "We're nearly there. I can see the light up ahead. I think we're going to make it". With renewed vigour, they sped towards the southern boundary of the forest. The air around them became lighter and lighter as they ran until, right in front of them, Lunamor spotted a wider gap between two trees. Directly beyond it was an open expanse of clear blue sky. Lunamor had never seen such a welcome sight and, drawing more air into his lungs, he put his head down and continued his sprint to safety.

It was then that Rendol gave a piercing and terrified scream. Terrible visions rushed through Lunamor's head. Visions of Rendol succumbing to the poisonous barbs of the olmflies. Visions of his lifeless, black eyes gazing vacantly into the canopy of the trees above. Visions of himself being their next target. Before Lunamor was able to react to the Skogner's cry of terror, he suddenly found himself hitting an invisible barrier strung between the two trees. Lunamor expected to be flung backwards into the path of the vicious olmflies but instead he stuck fast to the obstacle which had blocked his escape. Struggling wildly, Lunamor tried to free himself from what he now saw was an almost invisible web spun across the space between the two trees they had hoped to escape though. At the side of him, he became aware of the Skogner also desperately trying to free himself from the sticky strands.

In a matter of seconds, the only thing the two had succeeded in achieving was in turning so that they now faced into the forest. What they saw there caused the blood to freeze in their veins. Rendol gave out a low moan of despair. Hovering in front of them was the swarm of olmflies and now they had their prey exactly where they wanted it…

Chapter 10

Still panting heavily after their race for freedom through the forest, Lunamor and Rendol watched the olmflies hovering in a pyramid formation in front of them. Now that their prey was held captive, it didn't look like they were in any rush to attack. "What are we going to do?" asked Lunamor helplessly. He could feel the small Skogner quivering with fear at the side of him.

They seemed to be caught in gluey filaments which had been stretched backwards and forwards between the trees creating a spider web effect. Now that Lunamor was entangled in the tacky net he noticed that the trap was only visible in some lights. If he looked at it one way it looked as though Rendol was suspended in mid-air even though his wings were still but if he looked at it a different way he could see the trap which held them fast. Each strand was pale yellow and as thick as one of Lunamor's fingers. Coating the strands was a gooey substance which shone like droplets of dew glistening in the sun.

The olmflies suddenly increased their buzzing and, as one, they all inched closer to where their quarry hung defencelessly. Cringing backwards as far as they could, Lunamor and Rendol closed their eyes tight and waited for the inevitable sting of the olmflies' barbed tails. But it never came. Instead, the whistling buzz suddenly took on an urgency that hadn't been there before. It was an almost panicked sound as though the olmflies were communicating in frenzied tones. Lunamor, thinking that this was the end, wanted to face it bravely. He opened his eyes and was shocked to see the olmflies making a hasty retreat into the forest.

"They're leaving", said Lunamor with a sigh of relief to the Skogner, who seemed to have been rendered unusually speechless by the events of the last few minutes. "That can't be right", replied Rendol with uncertainty, "I've never seen olmflies give up a chase and they had us exactly where they wanted us. Why would they just leave?".
"I don't know," answered Lunamor, "but they certainly left in a hurry. It was almost as though they were scared of something".
"Well it isn't us they're scared…ow!" Rendol stopped speaking as he felt Lunamor's elbow dig sharply into his side. "Shh!" urged Lunamor, 'Listen!".

Rendol was about to protest when he too heard what had prompted Lunamor to nudge him so roughly. Coming up behind them they could hear the thud of heavy footsteps and an unusual dragging sound. This was accompanied by loud breathing which the two could feel, hot and smelly, on the backs of their necks. Frantically, they struggled against the sticky ropes that bound them but they were unable to see what it was that was approaching. "I think we know why the olmflies made such a quick getaway anyway," muttered Rendol under his breath.

Without warning, a razor sharp claw sliced through the netting of the web right between Lunamor and Rendol's faces. As the claw passed less than a moon stone from his face, Lunamor just had time to notice that it was incredibly beautiful, pearlescent in colour, but also deadly sharp. Then the claw sliced again and then again, ripping away at the sticky substance that had held them against their will. Before they knew it, Lunamor and Rendol were both freed from their imprisonment in the trap and, as one, they slowly turned to face this new and terrible danger.

Stood before them was the most magnificent dragon imaginable. Its diamond shaped scales were the colours of all the crystals of the world and covered its entire body from its immense head all the way down to the tip of its lengthy tail. It was easily twice as tall as Lunamor and the sheer size of the creature in front of them should have terrified them both but there was something about its eyes that instantly made them feel safe. They were soulful eyes surrounded by long golden lashes and they gazed at Lunamor and Rendol kindly. Hesitantly, Lunamor stepped forward and said simply, "Thank you". The dragon blinked slowly and then nodded its great head once in acknowledgement. "You ruined my net," stated the dragon in an injured tone.
"This was your trap?" asked Rendol, angrily, "We almost died because of you! And what are you even hoping to catch, here at the edge of the forest, anyway?"

"I'm a Wind Speeder Dragon. The leathered night owls which fly in and out of the forest during the hours of darkness are a great delicacy," explained the dragon, "and now I'm going to have to weave my trap again otherwise I'll never catch anything". As it spoke, the Wind Speeder Dragon had begun to pull at a pale yellow strand which was hanging from an especially large scale underneath its long, flattened snout. The strand grew longer and longer and, as it did so, the dragon wrapped the lengthening filament around its paws. "We're sorry," said Lunamor, "We didn't mean to run into your trap. We didn't even see it. Please forgive us. My name is Lunamor and this is Rendol". The Wind Speeder Dragon gazed at Lunamor curiously for a few more minutes and then said, "I'm Frione. I live on the western border of this world with my fellow Wind Speeders. I think our leader, Shamol, would be very interested in talking to you, Lunamor". As Lunamor looked into the Wind Speeders' eyes they came to an understanding that had no need of words.

"Well that's nice isn't it?" huffed Rendol who was feeling a little put out by the attention Lunamor was receiving. Lunamor turned to the Skogner who was hovering dejectedly at his side. "I really appreciate everything you have done, Rendol. I couldn't have made it through Morupo without you. You really have taught me so much and I'll never, ever be able to thank you enough but your place is in the forest. I have to go on to find out who I am. I have to learn more of the prophecy and I can't do that if I stay here". Tears were silently trickling down Rendol's face and, giving a sudden sob, he threw himself into Lunamor's arm. The two embraced for many minutes and then, reluctantly, Lunamor held the Skogner away from him. Rendol fluttered sadly for a few more minutes and then turned away and headed into the forest. He was soon lost to sight in the black shadows caused by the trees.

Lunamor looked after the retreating back of the Skogner for a few more seconds and then turned to face the Wind Speeder, Frione. The dragon turned its back and Lunamor watched as it began unfurling two enormous wings of the most glorious rainbow of colours. The wings seemed to change colour as the light hit them so that one minute they were red, then blue, then green, then yellow. Giving a sigh, Frione abandoned the sticky filaments it had been gathering and let them drift to the floor. "Climb on then," said Frione and he indicated his back with a jerk of his head. Lunamor, looking very unsure, managed to step up onto the dragon's back by climbing up its tail and settled himself between the two wings, his spear tucked under his arm. By now the wings had completely unfurled and made a sheltered space for Lunamor to nestle. Without warning, the Wind Speeder beat its wings twice and then they were high up in the air and flying swiftly towards the west.

Chapter 11

Far below, trees, rocks, streams and valleys all raced by as the Wind Speeder dragon flew at a pace that had been previously unimaginable to Lunamor. He kept his eyes squeezed tightly shut and his face pressed into the cold scales of Frione's neck not daring to look at the blurred ground over which they flew so rapidly. Occasionally, he could feel the dragon tip his body to left or right as he made slight adjustments to the direction he was flying in. At these times, Lunamor clung on even tighter, fearing that he would plummet to the ground.

After a short while, Lunamor felt the dragon slow his speed a little and then Frione spoke, "We have almost reached the western brink of Orokuvar. It is a wonderful sight and you are quite safe so why don't you take a look about you?". Reluctantly, Lunamor straightened from the hunched position he had been sitting in but kept a tight hold of the larger scales on Frione's back. What he saw was such a spectacular sight that it completely took his breath away.

Far below, the land dipped and rose in gentle valleys of the lushest and greenest grass Lunamor had ever seen. Crisscrossing the vibrant green were streams which, from this great height, looked like dribbles of molten silver. But it wasn't the sight below that had so enraptured Lunamor rather than what he saw before him. They had almost reached the westernmost edge of Orokuvar and Lunamor gazed in wonder at the sharp line dividing the green of the meadow and the blackness of the empty space beyond their world. As they flew closer, Lunamor watched as dozens of Wind Speeder dragons leapt off the brink and disappeared over the edge into the nothingness below only to rear back up into the velvet darkness. The pale crystal shades of their scales was in stark contrast to the inky black arena in which the dragons showed off their incredible grace, speed and agility.

"Hold on tight," instructed Frione as he began a steady descent down towards the ground. The closer they got to the land below, the more detail Lunamor was able to make out. Scattered along the very edge of the border were a variety of colourful tents of all shapes and sizes. Some were circular with a large central pole to hold them up; some were clearly made for just one dragon and still others seemed to be open at the sides and looked to hold stores of supplies. One tent stood apart from all the others, a little way from the edge, and was the largest of all. Its canvas was a vivid mix of topaz blue and ruby red and looked to be made of some kind of silky material. It was towards this tent that Frione flew.

With surprisingly little sound, the Wind Speeder dragon landed with a soft thud a short distance away from the large tent. Due to the fast speeds the dragon was able to fly, the journey had taken little more than 10 minutes. Lunamor slid down from the dragon's back and surreptitiously checked his inner pocket to make sure the geode was still tucked away safely. Then, he looked at Frione questioningly. "You say that your leader would be interested in speaking to me, why?" The Wind Speeder seemed to consider Lunamor's question for some time and then answered simply, "The prophecy speaks of you". He then began walking towards the tent in front of them, his long tail dragging across the ground behind him. Lunamor hurried to catch up.

As they reached the tent, an opening suddenly appeared as some of the silky material was gathered together and pulled to one side by some unseen hand. Frione stopped at the opening and gestured that Lunamor should step inside. Uncertain of what he would find there, Lunamor entered, leaving behind the bright sunshine of the day. Inside, the tent was not as gloomy as Lunamor had expected. The canvas of the tent seemed to allow an unnatural amount of light through and so the interior was well lit albeit with a purplish glow. Seated amongst a pile of huge cushions was the leader of the Wind Speeder dragons, Shamol.

Shamol was dazzling to look at. His scales seemed to glow from within highlighting the brilliance of their crystal colours. As Lunamor stood before the leader, he was speckled with sparks of light which reflected back from the dragon in front of him. Shamol beckoned with one long, elegant pearlescent claw so that Lunamor felt forced to move closer. The leader of the Wind Speeder dragons then gestured to a smaller pile of cushions to the side of him indicating that Luanmor should sit. Lunamor hesitated for only a moment and then walked over to the cushions and gratefully sank into them.

"You are the Crystal Bearer, are you not?" asked the dragon in a voice which was remarkably soft and gentle considering his size. Lunamor was unsure how to answer this question. Was he the Crystal bearer? Could he possibly have anything to do with the prophecy Rendol had told him of? Instead of answering the question, Lunamor responded with questions of his own, "What makes you think I am the Crystal Bearer? What do you know of me? What do you know of my people?". Shamol gave a sudden chuckle which sounded as though a number of bells had been struck all at once. His immense stomach shuddered as he laughed causing the shimmering scales on his chest to sparkle and scatter shards of light all around the tent. "You hold the greatest of powers in the whole of Orokuvar and yet you know not who you are," declared the dragon, suddenly becoming very serious, "Well, there will be time enough to share with you what we know. The suns will be setting shortly so let us find you something to eat and somewhere you can rest for the night. We will speak again in the morning and I will tell you the tale we have to tell".

Before he knew what was happening, Lunamor had been escorted out into the gradually darkening day, guided by two more Wind Speeder dragons. The weary traveller was taken to a smaller tent which was positioned beside Shamol's majestic shelter. Suddenly overcome with a feeling of great fatigue, he was thankful when he was provided with a hot, steaming bowl of broth and then left to himself. Lunamor quickly drank the broth and, with barely any awareness of his surroundings, settled himself back onto the cushions which had been laid out for him. Without even one last conscious thought he sank into a deep sleep.

Chapter 12

Shortly after the two suns had risen, Lunamor awoke feeling disoriented. Beneath him was a pile of fragrant cushions made of moon worm silk which were filled with sweet smelling grasses. Above him, stretched the silky fabric of a tent which was a glorious yellowy orange almost the exact same shade as the setting sun. Through the thin material, he could feel the sun's rays warm his skin. As he came more fully awake, he remembered the events of the day before and his unsettling meeting with Shamol, the leader of the Wind Speeder dragons. Hopefully, today would be the day that he got some answers and that everything might finally start to make sense.

Feeling refreshed, Lunamor rose from the cushions and looked around for the opening in the tent's side. Eventually, he found the pull cord which, when he tugged it, gathered some of the tent's material together and created an opening for him to pass through. There, before him, was a hive of activity. Wind Speeder dragons moved this way and that in a kind of organised chaos. Some carried huge platters of food the likes of which Lunamor had never seen before: giant fish whose golden scales glinted in the sun; vegetables that were completely alien to Lunamor and delicious looking fruits of all colours of the rainbow. Other dragons were stringing up bunting between the tents; each small triangle was decorated with the image of two dragon wings. Still others were setting up a table so vast that Lunamor could barely see the furthest end of it. Every dragon seemed to be busy at their task and took no notice of the stranger in their midst.

Unsure of where to go or what to do, Lunamor stood in the opening of his tent watching the comings and goings of the Wind Speeders. At that moment, he spotted Frione landing gracefully a short distance away. In his claws the dragon was gripping three dead birds. Instead of feathers they had rust coloured, leather-like skin and Lunamor assumed they were the leathered night owls Frione had been hoping to catch the day before. He held his hand up in a quick wave and, spotting him, the dragon ambled over.

"I left before sunrise this morning to visit one of my other traps. Luckily, I was able to catch these," said Frione as he held up the birds he was clutching in his claws, "As I told you, these are a great delicacy and the feast would not be a feast without them".
"What is the feast for?" asked Lunamor curiously.
"It's our annual Wind Speeder Master tournament today. The fastest and most daring dragons compete for the prestige of knowing they possess the greatest flying skills," explained Frione, "Afterwards, we hold a spectacular banquet to celebrate our most accomplished flyers. Speaking of which, I better get these birds over to the fire pit so that they can be cooked". Frione gestured that Lunamor should follow him and, together, they wove in and out of the busy dragons preparing for the tournament and its subsequent celebration.

As they moved further away from the brink, and the hustle and bustle that could be found there, Lunamor spotted the fire pit Frione had spoken of. It consisted of a huge hole which had been dug into the ground and then filled with the trunks of a large number of trees. The tree trunks had been heaped in a pile in the centre of the enormous pit. As Lunamor looked on, he saw four dragons carrying the biggest fire crystal he had ever seen. They heaved it over the edge of the fire pit and, the moment it struck the dry wood, there was an almighty whoosh and the hole was filled with a roaring fire. For a moment, Lunamor was blinded by the bright light of the flames. When he was able to see again, he saw that the four dragons were now laying a number of spits across the hole upon which were strung a variety of animal carcasses. They then settled down to watch the meat roast, turning the spits occasionally to ensure that they cooked evenly.

Frione approached one of the four dragons hunched over his spit and handed over the leathered night owls he had caught. Lunamor hung back and watched as the dragons exchanged a few words. Feeling extremely uncomfortable, he tried to appear as though he hadn't noticed the way the four dragons stared unashamedly at him. When they had finished speaking, Frione returned to Luanmor's side. "Come, let's go and see Shamol, he is expecting you," said Frione who turned and walked away from the fire pit and the four dragons who looked on with interest. With a final look back, Lunamor followed.

Before long they had arrived at the magnificent tent which sheltered Shamol. As before, the opening in the tent suddenly appeared as if by magic. Lunamor entered the confines of the tent and was once again confronted by the impressive sight of the Wind Speeder dragons' leader perched upon his throne of cushions. "I take it you slept well, Crystal Bearer," said Shamol as he signalled for Lunamor to take a seat to the side of him. "You have arrived at a good time, you will be able to witness the incredible skills of some of our most fearless flyers".
"I'd like that," said Lunamor as he settled himself on the smaller heap of cushions. He didn't much like being referred to as Crystal Bearer as he felt certain that Shamol must be mistaken. It couldn't possibly be true that he, an exile of Caamond, should be so important as to be referred to in an ancient prophecy.

"Since leaving Caamond, I have travelled a long way. Exiled by those I thought were my people, I'm on a journey to try to discover where I truly belong," explained Lunamor, "and I think that you may be able to help me". Shamol studied Lunamor intently, almost as though he was trying to search the travellers inner thoughts. Then, he began to speak.

It all started with a shower of stars.

The Wind Speeder dragons of the time had been diving from the brink and practising their acrobatics in the open space beyond Orokuvar. It is a favourite pastime of the Wind Speeders and they never tire of it. On this day, they had continued to practise well past sunset and so flew from our darkened world into the blackness, barely able to distinguish land from the empty vastness beyond the brink. Deciding it was time to stop for the day, they had all landed safely when suddenly an odd light appeared in the south east. It flickered strangely and the dragons did not know what they were witnessing.

As they watched, the light drew closer and closer until the gathered dragons could see that it was in fact a shower of stars which rained down from the heavens above. From their vantage points the dragons were unable to see where these stars made contact with the ground or if, indeed, they even did. Astonished, the dragons looked on as the stars seemed to sweep past their territory, move over the forest of Morupo and then suddenly disappear.

That night the dragons gathered around their leader, Hergal, and talked of what they had seen. They were unsettled by what they had observed and unsure what it meant for them and their world. There was a great deal of anxiety among the dragons and some of them wanted to leave the brink to go investigate. Hergal would not hear of this. He suggested that they sleep on it and discuss the matter further the next day.

The following day, the dragons were unable to talk of anything else and, as they went about their day to day tasks, they clustered in small groups to discuss the stars which had rained down so mysteriously. It was around midday, when a watchful dragon spotted a dark mass moving across the grasslands. From their position on the lip of Orokuvar, the dragons couldn't make out what it was that was travelling with such purpose towards the forest of Morupo. Hergal promptly sent out a party of his fastest dragons to take a closer look.

Once the dragons were directly overhead they saw that it was in fact a group of five voyagers. They travelled on foot and were armed with spears. They didn't spot the dragons, far above them, but, with their exceptional eyesight, the dragons were able to make out the features of these travellers. They looked just like you Lunamor. As the dragons looked on, the group below them entered the depths of the forest and then were lost to sight.

The dragons who had been sent to investigate reported back to Hergal what they had seen. For many, many moons the Wind Speeders' leader considered what he should do. The Wind Speeder dragons didn't often travel far beyond Morupo but Hergal felt the need to follow where the travellers had gone. It was for this reason that he sent out another group of Wind Speeder dragons to try to discover the travellers' destination and to maybe discover the meaning of the shower of stars that had come ahead of the appearance of these strangers.

A group of three dragons set out immediately. It didn't take them long to fly over the broad stretch of forest and they soon reached the northern boundary of Morupo. From the edge of Morupo, they observed that the ground before them was dotted with patches of burnt grass. At the far northern edge of the world, the dragon's could just make out the northern boundary of Orokuvar and the blankness beyond. But it wasn't this northern boundary that caught their attention, or even the odd patches of scorched earth. What drew their attention most was the activity of the five travellers. In the time that Hergal had spent considering the potential dangers of sending out a scouting party, the five travellers had begun work on laying the foundations of what was clearly going to be a large building. In only a short time, they had begun to construct a building of stone unlike anything the dragons had ever seen before.

Lunamor hung on the dragons' every word. What Shamol had said seemed to support the story told to him by Rendol but it just didn't make sense to Lunamor. These travellers looked like him, yet the inhabitants of Caamond did not. He had been forced out of the city because he had continued to grow and because of the symbol on his neck. Yet, it appeared that the founding fathers of that city had been just like him once upon a time. Why was this not known by the Perpetuates? Why did they not recognise him as a descendent of these first Eternal Children? Surely, if they had known this, they would not have exiled him.

"I have heard a similar tale before, whilst I was travelling through the forest," explained Lunamor, "it appears that the Eternal Children you saw were following the shower of stars because of a prediction made by their ancestors". Shamol listened with interest. "You are clearly a descendent of these travellers, Lunamor, what you need to discover is what this prediction is that they spoke of".
"Earlier you called me Crystal Bearer. Why do you say this?" asked Lunamor. He was almost afraid to hear the answer but he knew that in order to move on with his journey he needed to hear what Shamol had to say.

"You carry a geode, do you not?" said Shamol, his eyes almost glistening with amusement. Lunamor looked shocked. How could the dragon possibly know this? He hadn't removed the geode from his pocket even once since his arrival at the brink of Orokuvar. Self-consciously, Lunamor patted his chest, reassuring himself that the geode was still securely in his pocket. He could feel its solidness through the thin fabric of his tunic and breathed a sigh of relief. "Don't worry, we have not taken it from you," reassured the dragon.
"Then how did you know about it?" exclaimed Lunamor.
"We Wind Speeders can feel its power. When Frione found you at the edge of the forest he knew at once that you carried this rarest of objects. We have waited a long time for you. A long, long time ago we were told of a prophecy by a Tugarl with one purpose to his life. This purpose was to ensure that those that mattered knew of your existence". At this, Lunamor glanced at Shamol in surprise. "You have heard of the prophecy already, I can tell," stated the dragon. "Then you must know that this prophecy refers to the geode which you now carry. We can feel its immense power like a pulse in our veins. You do not yet know what it is capable of, but you will. You will," declared Shamol with certainty.

As the dragon finished speaking, Frione hurried over and announced that the tournament was about to begin. "Come," said Shamol, "let's go watch the tournament. I can assure you you will see nothing like it on your travels". With that the leader of the Wind Speeder dragons led the way and Frione and Lunamor followed behind.

Chapter 13

Lunamor, Frione and the leader of the Wind Speeder dragons arrived at the edge of the brink just as the resonant sound of a gong echoed across the grasslands. This seemed to signal that the tournament would be starting shortly and the last few dragons hurried over to take their places. Shamol's stack of cushions had been moved outside for the day's events and he now settled himself comfortably on these. Frione and Lunamor took a seat on either side of him. From where they sat, they had an unobstructed view of the vibrant green of the brink which then plunged into the blackness of nothingness.

The gong sounded again and the gathered dragons fell silent expectantly. "Welcome, all, to our annual Wind Speeder Master tournament," announced Shamol, "Candidates, you have put yourselves forward as you think you have what it takes to be crowned Wing Speeder Master. This is your opportunity to show your speed, daring and creativity. Take flight and show us what you can do!". As he finished speaking, the crowd of dragons erupted, cheering and shouting the names of their favourite contestants. Lunamor looked on in bewilderment. Back in Caamond, the Eternal Children were fond of their rituals and celebrations of the moon phases but these were always very calm and sedate affairs. Nothing like the riot of colour and noise that he could see here.

The crowd suddenly fell silent and Lunamor watched as three dragons lined up on the edge of the brink. From his vantage point, right at the front, Lunamor could see the glint of determination in their eyes and the way their pearlescent claws hooked over the lip of the land. The sudden sounding of the gong spurred the dragons into action and they shot off into the inky vast space before them, tufts of grass flying up into the air as they went. Within seconds the dragons had disappeared, flying out and away from the brink and disappearing into the forbidding emptiness beyond. The dragons and Lunamor waited, breath held, for the three competitors to return. As Lunamor watched, he could see the pale forms of the trio of dragons appearing out of the gloom. They seemed to be neck and neck. With a sudden burst of energy, the smaller of the three dragons shot forward, reaching the edge of the brink first. She hit the ground hard and rolled three times, then jumped to her feet and gave a little mock bow. The crowd cheered enthusiastically.

"Flankrin: 1 point!" announced a voice. The smaller dragon, Flankrin, grinned at the crowd and then rejoined her two opponents. After a few moments to catch their breath the dragons lined up again, spacing themselves out along the edge. "The first to catch the leathered night owl will win the point," declared the voice again and Lunamor noticed that, to the right, stood an extremely large dragon holding a flapping night owl by its feet. Frione leant over and whispered, "There is a reason we set traps for these birds rather than trying to catch them ourselves". The bird was squawking loudly, its leathered wings snatching at the air as it tried to escape the dragon's clutches

The gong sounded again and the bird was released. Great leather wings spread wide, it hovered for a few seconds in the air and then swooped off into the black obscurity beyond. Without hesitation, two of the three dragons shot off after it but the larger of the three dragons hung back, lingering just above the brink. Lunamor wanted to ask Frione why the dragon hadn't gone after the bird but, before he had the chance, he noticed that the panicked night owl had flown back towards land. The larger dragon was ready for it and swooped upwards and into the path of the bird. As quick as a flash, the large dragon shot out her claw tipped paw and snatched her target, mid-flight, out of the air. She held it up above her head triumphantly as Flankrin and the other dragon returned empty handed. "Shanzor: 1 point!" shouted the voice.

"The next round is where the competitors get to show off their agility," explained Shamol, "It's my favourite part of the tournament. I was pretty good in this round myself, in my day". Lunamor nodded politely and looked on eagerly as the three competitors gathered around the dragon who appeared to be in charge of the day's events. "The dragon who has yet to win any points, Dlyn, is known for his dexterity. I'm sure this is where he will close the gap," said Frione confidently.

Once again, the three dragons took up their positions. Lunamor could see the concentration on their faces, possibly as they went over their sequence of moves in their minds. "They spend many moons practising," said Shamol, "so there is a lot invested in this part of the competition". The resounding sound of the gong was heard again and, gracefully this time, the dragons glided up into the air. Lunamor watched in awe as Flankrin, Dlyn and Shanzor twisted and twirled in the jetblack depths of the sky beyond the edge of the world. They swooped and swirled, soared and skated through the space beyond. Despite their size and bulk they were able to twist and turn, making sudden changes in direction, one minute twirling up and up and the next plunging downwards in a spiral. The congregation of dragons below, oohed and aahed as they watched these spectacular feats of daring.

As the gong signalled the end of the round the three competitors landed gracefully on the ground. The watching dragons went wild, cheering and shouting their excitement. Then all went quiet as Shamol rose to award the points. "As ever, we have just observed what truly makes us unique from all other dragons of Orokuvar. There are no others who can fly with the skill and dexterity shown here today. It is always a difficult job for me to have to choose between you but there is one clear winner in the agility round this year; Dlyn, I award you 3 points, Shanzor, I award you 2 points and Flankrin, I award you 1 point". As Shamol finished speaking, the mass of dragons again erupted with yelling and clapping in appreciation of the points that had been awarded.

"As we move onto our final round the scores stand as follows; Flankrin is in second place with 2 points, Shanzor and Dlyn are in joint first place with three points. The winner of this next and final round will be awarded 2 points and this will decide our winner," shouted the announcer excitedly. "This event is really dangerous," whispered Frione, "and it takes incredible bravery to be the victor in this round". Lunamor was about to ask more, when the noise of the gong reverberated through the air for the final time.

As one, the three dragons rose up into the sky, they hovered for a moment and then continued to rise higher and higher until they were lost to sight. Lunamor was unsure what to expect but then he heard it; a roaring sound as though wind was rushing through a tunnel. Still looking upwards, Lunamor saw that the three dragons were now plummeting down to the ground, their legs tucked in and snouts pushed forwards. Their wings were flattened against their backs so that, rather than flying, the dragons were in fact free falling towards the land. At any moment, Lunamor expected them to uncurl their wings and turn away from the hard ground but this didn't happen. Instead their speed seemed to increase and they came closer and closer to what would surely be a catastrophic impact. Suddenly, Shaynee reared off to one side and Lunamor finally understood what the aim of this round was. It seemed to be a test of nerve. Who would be the last to turn away from the fatal impact with the ground? Flankrin and Dlyn were now snout to snout and were mere moonstones away from collision. Just when Lunamor thought they were both surely going to hit the ground Dlyn twisted away followed seconds later by Flankrin.

The watching dragons jumped to their feet, shouting and cheering. The voice of the announcer declaring the winner was lost in the cacophony of sound. Shamol rose from his cushions and approached Flankrin. The leader of the Wind Speeders was handed a chain of silver so chunky it was easily twice as thick as Lunamor's arm. This was placed around Flankrin's neck. Then, the victor was escorted ceremoniously, by Shamol, to the feast that awaited them. The crowd of jubilant dragons followed closely behind and Lunamor found himself swept along with them.

Chapter 14

As the celebration feast began, Lunamor found himself seated to the left of a dragon who had been placed at the head of the table. Because of her prominent position at the table, Lunamor assumed that she must be the dragon leaders' mate. Her scales were so delicate and fine they were almost translucent and, atop her head, was perched a fine band of gold which had been inlaid with bevelled gems. As she turned her head to converse with the dragons around her, the precious stones caught the light, glimmering and sparkling.

At the opposite end of the table, Frione was seated beside Shamol. The two were deep in conversation and Lunamor, despite the chatter all around him, found himself feeling very alone. It seemed that everyone had a place where they belonged. Even Rendol, who had no family, knew where he had come from and had a place he could call home. Lunamor had once known that feeling of family; he had once felt like he belonged. As a young Eternal Child, he had been loved and protected by his Founder, Kuu, which made the isolation he now felt so much harder to bear. Their relationship wasn't a demonstrative one, as Eternal Children of Caamond are not known for their displays of affection, but Kuu showed his love in other ways. It was shown in the way Kuu really listened to Lunamor when he spoke; in the way Kuu lit the fire before Lunamor awoke so that he wouldn't be cold when he rose from his bed and finally it had been shown at the end when Kuu had warned him of what was to come.

As though sensing his melancholy mood, the beautiful dragon seated beside him suddenly turned and gazed right into his eyes. Like Frione's they were striking in the way they seemed to see right into the very core of him. He felt extremely exposed but at the same time understood in a way he had never been before, even by Kuu. As she studied him now, he knew she could feel how he felt and that she felt his overwhelming loneliness just as keenly as he did. She reached over and gently placed her claw tipped paw over his hand comfortingly; a solitary tear rolled down her snout and onto the table.

"You will find your place, Lunamor," said the dragon tenderly, "Your journey has only just begun. I may not have the power of your crystals and geodes, and I may not be able to make predictions like those of your race, but I do know that you will find yourself and when you do you will achieve the feelings of belonging you so desire". Lunamor didn't know why but, as she spoke these words, he believed everything she was telling him and he felt a lightening of his heart.

Feeling strangely better, he tucked into the feast before him, eating until his stomach hurt. Once the banquet had been demolished, the dragon beside him turned and asked him to escort her to her tent. They meandered in and out of the scattered tents as she introduced herself properly. She was called Yeni and confirmed that his intuition was right and that she was Shamol's mate. Finally, they arrived at a tent which was set slightly apart from the others. The opening of the tent was flanked by two statues which had been carved from highly polished marble of the palest pink. They were such great likenesses that it was immediately obvious they represented

Shamol and his partner Yeni. The sculptor had gone to great pains to ensure that every scale was intricately chiselled into the smooth stone and had even managed to capture the expressive eyes of the Wind Speeder dragons.

"Just wait here one moment," instructed Yeni politely and she then disappeared into the tent. Lunamor waited patiently, looking about him as dragons began to make their way to their own tents before night set in. It wasn't long before she had returned, carrying a small drawstring bag made of silk spun by the moon worms who descended on every available surface just once a year. "I want you to have these, Lunamor," said Yeni as she placed the bag gently in his hands. Lunamor pulled open the gathered opening at the top of the bag and was stunned to see that the pouch was filled with the pearlescent claws of the Wind Speeder dragons. He looked up at Yeni, confusion evident on his face. "As you can see, these are the claws of Wind Speeders. When a dragon passes away from this life their claws are saved. They have amazing healing properties and are not given away lightly. In fact, we have only once passed these into the hands of someone who is not a Wind Speeder and that was to the Tugarl who came and spoke of the prophecy".

Lunamor gazed in wonder at the claws nestled in the silky bag. They were at least three moon stones in length and were incredibly smooth. Their polished surfaces reflected the waning light of the setting suns as they shifted in Lunamor's hands. "I...I...I don't know what to say," stuttered Lunamor. He felt so incredibly honoured that he was at a loss for words. "You need say nothing, only go on your journey with true belief in your abilities. I know that you do not believe the tales you have been told but, if you are to succeed, you need to realise the true power of the geode you carry". With that, Yeni tenderly patted Lunamor on the shoulder and disappeared into her tent.

Lunamor pulled the drawstring bag closed and tucked it into his pocket, feeling the coolness of the geode against his skin as he did so. Maybe he did need to have a little more faith. He had survived this far and had come further than any other citizen of Caamond. As he thought this, he was filled with a feeling of pride at what he had accomplished so far. He returned to his tent and settled down to sleep for the night. He would continue his journey again tomorrow at first light.

Chapter 15

Lunamor woke early the next morning, keen to be on his way. Now that he had learnt as much as he was able to here, he was anxious to continue his journey. He left his tent and went in search of Fione so that he could say goodbye. All evidence of the previous day's festivities had gone and the dragons went about their day to day business.

Lunamor spotted one of the dragons who had worked at the fire pit the day before and approached him. "Do you know where I will find Frione?" he asked. The dragon looked a little awe-struck and Lunamor realised that word must have spread, amongst the dragons, of who Shamol and Yeni said he was. Finally the tongue tied dragon answered, "He is preparing for the journey so he is probably at the brink". Lunamor thanked him and set off towards the lip of land which separated solid ground from empty space. He wondered what journey the dragon meant.

When he arrived at the brink, he couldn't see Frione anywhere. Lunamor settled himself on the grass to wait. Sure enough, it wasn't long before the Wind Speeder dragon emerged out of the gloom. "Ah, Lunamor, you're up at last," said Frione in greeting as he landed nimbly in front of him. "Your friends said you were preparing for a journey," Lunamor explained, "They said I would find you here".
"Yes, I've come to feast on the qarab bugs which live in swarms just off the brink. They give us Wind Speeders the extra energy needed to fly further distances".
"Yes, but where are you going?" asked Lunamor.
"With you, of course," said the dragon in surprise.
"With me? Why?" Lunamor stared open-mouthed at Frione. He had not expected that the Wind Speeder would want to accompany him. "Shamol has asked me to take you to the boundary of our lands and I am privileged to have been asked. Our lands are vast and there is little in the way of food or water. You would starve to death before you reached Toku. It is less than a day's journey for me to carry you across the grasslands. We will get there by nightfall".

Lunamor realised that what Frione had said was sensible. It would be much quicker to fly with the dragon and probably much safer. He also didn't relish the thought that, soon enough, he would be on his own and so he was thankful for the company Frione would provide. "Thank you Frione," said Lunamor sincerely.

Both travellers were soon ready to depart and were eager to be off. Before leaving, Frione accompanied Lunamor to Shamol's tent. Once again, he entered the luxuriant confines and was faced with the majestic leader of the Wind Speeder dragons. "Thank you for everything you have shared with me," began Lunamor. "It is nothing," said Shamol, brushing off Lunamor's thanks. The dragon clasped Lunamor's hands between his great paws and held them tightly. "Go, be safe on your journey and fulfil your purpose. We are honoured to have been able to aid the one the prophecy speaks of".

Lunamor emerged from the tent, into the bright, early morning sunshine and found Frione waiting impatiently for him. As before, Lunamor climbed up onto Frione's broad back and held his spear clamped tightly to his side. This time though, as the dragon lifted into the air, Lunamor didn't hide his eyes in fear and, instead, took in the wondrous sight of the grasslands falling away below him. Just before the tents of the Wind Speeder dragons disappeared from sight, Lunamor spotted Yeni standing outside her own tent, set slightly apart from the others in respect of her position amongst the dragons. He watched as, snout tilted in the air, she waved one paw at him in goodbye. Lunamor lifted his hand to return the gesture and then, facing forward once more, he looked ahead to what the next part of his journey would bring.

Chapter 16

Wind Speeder and Eternal Child raced through the air together in a pairing that had never been seen before. Lunamor was unable to make out any of the dips and rises of the land below as it raced quickly past in a green blur. The two suns were still ascending the sky and the peak of the day had not yet arrived but still Lunamor could feel the suns, warm against his back. A slipstream of air brushed back his grey curls and he had to blink his eyes repeatedly as the wind caused tears to roll down his freckled cheeks. Every now and again, Frione would lift his head and indicate to Lunamor some feature of the land far below with a gesture of his paw.

As midday approached, Frione swept down to the ground and the two took the opportunity to stretch their legs. The Wind Speeder dragon had brought a small bag which had been strapped to his side as he flew, and he now emptied this out, producing a delicious feast of leftover roasted meats, sliced fruits and charred vegetables from the banquet the day before. Lunamor ate quickly and drank thirstily from the pouch of water that had also been included. This looked to have been made from the leathered skin of the night owl and was the same rust colour as the birds Frione had caught for the feast. As he drained the last of the water from it, Frione gestured that Lunamor should keep hold of the water pouch so he tucked it into the bundle strapped to his back.

Looking around him, Lunamor was unable to see anything other than the open plains of the grasslands as far as the eye could see in every direction. Curious about where the next part of his journey would take him he asked, "What is beyond your grasslands?". The dragon finished with the piece of meat he had been eating and used the tip of his claw to prise a morsel of meat from between two of his dome shaped teeth before answering. "The land beyond ours is called Toku. It means 'death rocks'. We Wind Speeders don't go beyond our borders and the terrain of Toku is not one we would dare venture into. You will see when we arrive that it is not somewhere someone would want to settle. Beyond Toku, you will be able to see the rise of the terrible mountain ranges of Kriolk. These are at the very southern edge of Orokuvar and appear to be the direction in which you say your geode is guiding you," said the dragon, as he began packing up the remaining food into the bag. "If we are going to make the border of Toku before nightfall we need to make haste". After hearing what Frione had to say about Toku, Lunamor wasn't sure if he was in any rush to get there but he reluctantly got to his feet and helped Frione to clear away the last of their meal.

Up in the air once again, Lunamor dwelled on what Frione had said. As an Eternal Child of Caamond, he had never heard of Toku or of the mountains of Kriolk and so, instead, his imagination conjured up images of the hideous and terrifying beasts that might want to stalk him through the wilderness. Creatures that he would have no chance of defending himself against. If the Wind Speeder dragons, who were formidable in size, were terrified of Toku then what chance did he have? He could only hope that there really was some hidden power within his lilac crystal and the geode he carried. Or he may never reach his destination.

Although Frione was able to fly at incredible speed, the journey was still a long one and, at times, the gentle rocking motion of the dragon's wings as they lifted up and then dropped down again lulled Lunamor so much he would find himself drifting into sleep. It was only the sudden jerk, as he began to slide from the dragon's back, that jolted him awake and caused him to quickly grab onto the large scales at the back of Frione's neck.

Night was approaching, and colour was beginning to leech from the day when, far on the horizon, Lunamor spotted the mountain range Frione had spoken of. Even from this distance, Lunamor could see that the mountains were incredibly tall. They towered up into the sky, the peak lost in a haze of cloud. The red rock of the mountain face glowed amber in the light of the setting suns in stark contrast to the fading blue light of the day. In the foreground, Lunamor noticed an expanse of rock which reached out from the mountain's base, covering a vast area of land with its gnarled and stumpy fingers. "Toku," Lunamor heard Frione shout over the sound of the wind rushing past his ears. Lunamor shivered but wasn't sure if that was from the rapidly cooling air or because of the menacing looking rocks he was confronted by.

Frione flew on, drawing closer and closer to the point where luscious green grass ended and jutting rocks began. Finally, the Wind Speeder dragon began to make his descent and landed with a soft thump on the grass not far from where the lands of Toku began. It was only when Lunamor slid off the dragon's back, that he realised the rocky blanket he had seen from above, actually consisted of thousands of unique rock formations crowded close together. In between were narrow gaps which would accommodate Lunamor but would never have admitted the Wind Speeder dragon who was much bulkier.

As Lunamor stood, gazing in awe at the grotesque gallery of rocky statues, he became aware of the strong wind which buffeted at him, dragging his clothing this way and that and whipping at his hair. He squinted his eyes tightly shut against the fine dust of sand and grit which was being blown into his face by constant blasts of cold air. "Millions and millions of moons ago, the mountains of Kriolk were much, much higher," explained Frione, "But the river, which used to flow this way, carried much of the loose sand and grit down the mountain face, where it gathered to form a delta. Since then, the harsh winds which blow across the delta have carved the rocks into queer and unnatural shapes".

By now, the suns had started to sink lower in the sky and the world around them was quickly becoming darker. The wind whistled eerily between the rocks and caused the hairs on the back of Lunamor's neck to stand up on end. Frione looked concerned as he tilted his head back to look up at the sky above and said apologetically, "I'm afraid that I have to head straight back; there is a storm brewing and it wouldn't do for me to still be in the air when it hits". Lunamor had assumed that the darkening of the skies had been because of the setting of the suns and hadn't noticed what the dragon had seen. Huge, roiling black clouds had gathered towards the south-west border and appeared to be creeping up on them like a silent, oily black monster. As he watched, a flash of lightning lit up the clouds from the inside and the shadows of the jagged rocks next to which they stood seemed to jump out at Lunamor as though trying to snatch at him.

Lunamor thanked the Wind Dragon for everything he had done including saving him from the olmflies and bringing him this far on his journey and, as Frione lifted into the air, Lunamor hoped that he would one day be able to repay the kindness of Frione and all of the other Wind Speeder dragons. The lone traveller stood in the darkness, with the wind pushing and pulling at him, and watched as the dragon became a distant speck. Finally, starting to chill from the continuous gale that pummelled at him, Lunamor turned away and set about making a fire using his fire crystal. He wasn't ready to face the perils of Toku yet and certainly not during the blackness of night. Despite the fact that he had ridden rather than having to walk, Lunamor was so tired that he was fast asleep as soon as he had laid his head upon his small bundle. It was for this reason that he remained blissfully unaware of the numerous pairs of glinting eyes hidden amongst the rocks, which reflected back the light of his fire, and watched him as he slept.

Chapter 17

Lunamor awoke at the first light of day to the realisation that he was cold. His body shivered uncontrollably as the icy winds tried to burrow their way under the folds of his clothing. The black clouds from the night before were now directly overhead and Lunamor felt the first few spots of rain strike his upturned face. A rumble of thunder was quickly followed by a flash of lightning which zigzagged across the sky. Another boom, this time louder, spurred Lunamor into action and he quickly packed up his bundle and shrugged it onto his back.

As though the clouds had suddenly been squeezed by the hand of some invisible giant, a deluge of rain began to fall on Lunamor. He snatched up his spear and reluctantly headed into the shelter of rocks provided by Toku. The path between the rocks was narrow but he was able to walk fairly comfortably, only having to turn side on occasionally to squeeze through the smallest gaps. The close proximity of the rocks formed a natural shelter against the slanting rain and dulled the sound of the torrential downpour so that all Lunamor could hear was a muted thumping overhead.

Now that Lunamor was amongst the rocks, he was able to take a closer look at the strange formations surrounding him. Some of them had been formed into thin and twisted shapes which pointed up, dagger-like, into the air, the peaks having been whittled by the wind into a needle sharp point. Some of the formations consisted of larger, more rounded boulders, which balanced precariously upon tiny plinths of stone; But Lunamor edged around these ones nervously. But the formations that disturbed Lunamor the most were the ones that almost looked like the sand blasted carcasses of strange beasts or creatures. His imagination ran wild as visions of hideous beasts replaced the motionless rocks to lash out at him with spiny tails and snapping jaws. As he squeezed a path through the hulking figures he caught sight of things moving, out of the corner of his eye, only to turn swiftly and find that it was in fact just another oddly shaped boulder. These rocks appeared to take on a lifelike appearance with malformed skulls, deformed and contorted bodies and reaching claw-like hands.

It was gloomy amongst the rocks, a result of overhanging shelves of rock blocking out the light, but also because of the unnaturally darkened skies caused by the storm raging on above him. All of a sudden, Lunamor felt freezing fingers creeping across his feet and, looking down, he saw a rivulet of water running over the inadequate footwear he wore. It took a moment for Lunamor to make sense of what he was seeing but he soon realised that the heavy rainwaters must be washing down the mountainside and then flowing away between the rock formations of Toku. Quickly, Lunamor snatched the flask from his pack and stooped down to fill the leather pouch with fresh water. Who knew when he would next be able to refill it.

Lunamor waded on through the waters which now reached almost to his ankles. The force of the current, and uneven stones and pebbles hidden under the water's surface, caused him to stumble occasionally and so he used his hands to support himself against the stones on either side of him. Without warning, Lunamor felt the ground give way beneath him and he screamed aloud as he found himself sliding headfirst down a steeply sloping incline. Grabbing vainly at outcroppings of stone as he fell, his descent was only stopped when he reached the bottom and landed, with a splash, in a small pool of water. Lunamor looked around him and, with a feeling of dread, saw that he was now sitting in a deep well formed completely out of rock.

Getting shakily to his feet, Lunamor looked up at the rim of the deep depression and realised that the ledge of rock which rimmed the hole was way beyond the reach of his grasping fingers. As he watched, water continued to stream into the well and the water level, which had been just above his ankles, was now fast approaching the level of his knees. Lunamor felt panic beginning to rise within him. How was he going to get out of here? He walked over to the nearest wall and attempted to find purchase with his fingers and toes but the steep facades were formed of the hard rock of Toku and were glassy smooth. He scrabbled frantically at the wall but stopped when he realised that this was futile. By now the water had reached his hips and his teeth were chattering with the cold.

A deep depression fell over Lunamor. This was where it was going to end for him. He had been exiled, survived the dangers of Morupo and learnt much about where his ancestors, the true Eternal Children, had come from. He had heard incredible tales of the prophecy and, deep within himself, had almost begun to believe that he might just be the Crystal Bearer. But what good was that all going to do him now? He was going to drown here and nobody would ever know what had happened to him: not Kuu, not Rendol, not Shamol or Yeni or Frione. Not even the Perpetuates would have the satisfaction of knowing that they had succeeded in ridding the world of him completely.

Lunamor was jolted out of his melancholy thoughts as he became aware of a pulsing against his chest. So great was his despondency that at first it did not register with him that the throbbing he was feeling was not the terrified beating of his heart but was, in fact, the geode he carried with him. By the time he realised what he was feeling, the geode was vibrating insistently as though aware of the imminent danger its owner was in. With shaking hands, Lunamor pulled the geode out of his tunic pocket. The vibrations stopped instantly and, instead, the geode began to emit a ghostly, purple light. Acting on the instincts that had served him well before, Lunamor held the geode above his head with the flat, polished surface facing up to the sky.

Nothing happened. Lunamor felt as though he had failed some insurmountable test. How could he have possibly had the audacity to think that he actually was the Crystal Bearer? What right did he have to think that he, a nobody, could possibly be as important as he had stupidly started to believe he might be? The water was now above his shoulders but Lunamor remained standing with his arms outstretched above him and droplets of water bouncing off the flat surface of the geode like a shower of diamonds. Then, an amazing thing happened. The deep chasm Lunamor found himself trapped within suddenly filled with a dazzling lilac light. Looking down, Lunamor realised that this radiated from the crystal around his neck as well as from the geode held above his head. The strange glow seemed to take on real substance and Lunamor could almost feel the light gather around him to embrace him warmly.

Before he knew what had happened, he was rising out of the hole, as though the beacon of light was a tunnel through which he could walk. He rose above the edge of the rapidly filling reservoir of water and found that he was able to step forward onto the solid ledge of rock which surrounded the prison he had been trapped within.

As soon as his feet touched solid ground, the light vanished like a candle being blown out and the previous gloom returned. Lunamor should have been soaked through to the skin but strangely his clothes were now completely dry and the wind that tunnelled between the rocks did not seem to chill his skin as it had done before. His whole body seemed to throb with an immense power that he had not felt before and,for the first time, Lunamor truly believed that he was the Crystal Bearer. His destiny was set for something great. He truly mattered and his purpose was greater than that of all who walked the many corners of Orokuvar. Although Lunamor felt empowered by the realisations he had come to, he was overcome by the responsibility he now shouldered.

Chapter 18

With the rain still falling heavily above, and the storm clearly set to last for a while yet, Lunamor continued his journey into the depths of Toku. Whatever power he had been able to harness from the geode he carried, had stayed with him and the searching winds no longer bothered him. His body continued to tingle peculiarly as though the crystals's power was fizzing through his veins but it wasn't an unpleasant feeling. He welcomed the energy it seemed to inject him with and his stride was confident even as he moved further into the darkened maze of Toku. He felt fearless and unbeatable and, despite the fact that his journey was now being directed by an ancient prophecy and the powers of a geode he hadn't previously even known existed, he felt as though he was the master of his own destiny.

Eventually though he did start to tire and he realised that he had walked and walked without once stopping to rest. Although he still felt the warmth provided by the geode, the energy that had kept him going so far failed him now and he slumped to the ground in exhaustion. In a blurry haze of fatigue, Lunamor just had time to strike the Fire Crystal to start a decent fire, slide his crystal into the neck of his tunic out of sight and clasp his spear close to his side before sleep overcame him.

Lunamor's sleep was deep and, despite the experiences of the past few days, dreamless. The flames of the fire wavered in the strong winds that continued to blow but the fire stayed lit as a result of the power of the Fire Crystal which controlled it. All around him, towered the monoliths of Toku like a silent audience of monsters observing him sleep. But then, in the bleakness of the shadows, countless pairs of eyes began to appear, unblinking, to study the curious spectacle before them. They inched silently closer but remained hidden within the gloom.

Abruptly, Lunamor jerked awake. It wasn't that he had heard his soundless visitors, but a prickle of fear that somebody was watching him that had pulled him violently from his sleep. He jumped to his feet and raised his spear high, ready to defend himself against whatever lurked, hidden, amongst the rocks. But the gleaming eyes didn't move, they didn't blink, they just continued to stare straight at Lunamor. Lunamor stared back.

Shifting the spear from one hand to the other, Lunamor considered his options. It didn't appear as though the owners of the eyes intended to harm him as they would have attacked whilst he slept, however, Lunamor felt too unnerved to go back to sleep knowing that unseen creatures were waiting in the darkness watching him. He slowly reached down and picked up his Fire Crystal from where it lay near the fire. Slowly slipping one hand into his pocket he pulled out his knife and, without making any sudden movements, stuck the blade against the crystal. This caused the fire crystal to spring into life and a beam of light chased away the shadows which gathered around him and revealed the midnight visitors who surrounded him.

Scattered on outcroppings of rock, all around him, were giant beetles. Their shells were mottled grey with flecks of silver which enabled them to blend in easily with the stones around them. As the light exposed them to Lunamor's gaze, they didn't move away but instead seemed to edge slightly closer in a silent, slithering movement. It appeared that, instead of legs, they had one large foot, like a snail and Lunamor noticed that they left behind a faintly shimmering trail across the rocks as they moved. The eyes that he had been able to see glinting in the darkness were held up on two long stalks and they now stared steadily back at this strange creature standing in their midst.

Although he was surrounded, Lunamor did not feel any fear at the presence of the weird beetles. It was as though they were curious about the creature who had dared to venture through Toku. They gazed unwaveringly at him, their eyes swivelling on the long stalks which held the gleaming orbs at least 8 moonstones above the hard carapace of their shells. As if on some unspoken command, the beetles suddenly all turned, as one, and slid down the faces of the rocks they had perched atop. They then slipped across the rocky floor and disappeared out of sight. Lunamor watched in amazement as, one by one, the beetles all disappeared from sight, the silver specks of their shells twinkling like stars as they moved.

Seating himself next to the fire again, Lunamor felt uneasy. Why had the beetles disappeared so suddenly? He hadn't done anything to make them scared but that was the impression that he got. Their sudden retreat was almost as though they were fleeing some unseen predator. He just had time to consider this when he felt, rather than heard, the first signs of something quickly approaching. Whatever it was made no attempt to hide its arrival and tiny pebbles and stones on the floor around him began to skitter across the ground as the vibrations of pounding feet caused them to dance. Lunamor jumped to his feet and peered into the darkness fearfully. As well as being able to feel the tremors through the floor, he could now hear the thumping of footsteps coming towards him at a run. Snatching up his Fire Crystal, his spear and his bundle Lunamor ran in the same direction the beetles had disappeared in.

Holding the Fire Crystal aloft, Lunamor could just make out the slimy trail of the beetles as he ran and, not knowing what else to do, he followed the silvery path before him. Panic spurring him on, he dodged around the jagged rocks, grazing his shoulder on one boulder which jutted far out into his path. He rounded a particularly large formation in front of him just in time to see a steady stream of the beetles disappearing into a narrow aperture between two rocks. With a quick glance over his shoulder, Lunamor quickly followed.

He found himself in a cave which had been formed naturally by the rivers that had flowed through here. The cave was made of extremely hard stone and, where the softer stone had been washed away, the resulting effect was of a hollow in the centre of the massive boulder. The beetles were gathered across every available surface but Lunamor didn't have time to think about these. Instead, he quickly put out his Fire Crystal and then peeked through the narrow gap he had just about been able to squeeze through.

The pounding feet came closer causing clouds of dust and tiny pebbles to drift down from the overhanging rocks. Lunamor crouched in terror and waited for whatever monster approached to reveal itself. What he saw caused him to put one hand over his mouth to stop the gasp of horror from escaping his lips. Although not large, the creatures that came into sight were still much bigger than Lunamor. They ran on all fours and their reflexes were so great that they were easily able to dodge every obstacle in their way. Crazed eyes looked out of terrifying faces and Lunamor's gaze was drawn to the rows of snarling, snapping teeth which sprayed strings of saliva in every direction. The beasts were skeletal in appearance with their blackened skin stretched taut across the bones. As they ducked in and out of the closely gathered rocks which blocked their path, Lunamor could see the muscles and tendons working underneath the skin.

From his hiding place, Lunamor watched as first one, then two, then many more of the beasts ran past; so many that the scared Eternal Child lost count. It didn't appear as though these creatures hunted by smell as none of them glanced in Lunamor's direction but, nevertheless, he remained motionless, hardly breathing, until the creatures were out of sight. When he could no longer hear the echo of their pounding feet he turned his back to the crevice and slid to the floor. Considering the fact that these terrible creatures were moving in the same direction Lunamor wished to travel, he decided that it would be best to stay where he was for the night and give the beasts time to get well ahead of him. With any luck, he wouldn't come across them again. Wearily, he lowered himself down to the floor of the cave and despite the many eyes which continued to stare at him, he was soon fast asleep.

Chapter 19

The next morning Lunamor awoke feeling stiff. He had slept curled up in an unnatural position and now, as he straightened, his back and legs cracked in protest. At some point during the night, the beetles must have felt safe enough to leave the confines of the cave and Lunamnor now found that he was all alone. Taking confidence from this fact, he squeezed himself through the narrow opening and used a few shards of his crystal to find his bearing again. Once the geode had helped him to pinpoint the southern direction he needed to be heading in, he began to walk.

After only a few steps, he began to notice what looked like the white fur of an animal which had gathered up against the bottom of rocks where the wind couldn't quite reach. The further he went, the more of the white fur there was until the whole of the narrow trail between the rocks was covered with it. With every step Lunamor took, he sent miniature white clouds up into the air so that it felt as though he was walking through a blizzard of snow. He continued on, fur clinging to his clothing and hair, curious as to what creature had left behind this mysterious trail.

As he turned another corner, he came upon a strange sight. Growing from a crack in one of the rock formations was the first sign of plant life he had seen since entering Toku. A solitary ray of sunlight seemed to have managed to find a path through the towering stones and shone, like a spotlight, upon the plant. Feasting on the frilled leaves of the tenacious plant was what looked like a small ball of white fluff. It was only because the ball of fluff moved, and because of the fact he could hear the quiet munching sounds it made, that Lunamor was able to tell that this was in fact a living creature. As it became aware of his presence it lifted its head and turned to face Lunamor. Specks of green leaf were stuck to a trunk-like appendage which it seemed to use as a mouth and it blinked huge, startled eyes at Lunamor. Then, tiny wings appeared from the thick white fluff and it flew off between the statues of stone, scattering puffs of fur in every direction.

Lunamor's stomach gave a loud growl and he realised how hungry he was; he hadn't eaten since he had shared the leftovers of the banquet with Frione. He approached the strange plant growing out of the cracks of the rock. Tiny bite marks had been taken out of many of the leaves but some of the smaller leaves remained untouched. Surely, if the curious little creature he had just seen could eat these, then they would be fine for him too. Cautiously, Lunamor reached out and plucked a few of the younger shoots from the plant. He sniffed at them with uncertainty; their sweet fragrance caused Lunamor to salivate and, unable to hold back any longer, he crammed them into his mouth. He chewed and swallowed and then washed the small mouthful down with a swig of water from his pouch. He had eaten no more than one small mouthful however he oddly felt completely satisfied. He plucked the remaining untouched leaves and folded them into his bundle for later and then continued on his way.

He hadn't gotten very far when a wave of dizziness swept over him and, clutching in vain at the rocks around him, Lunamor dropped to his knees. He swayed there, helplessly, for a few moments and then tumbled over onto his back. Immobile, he lay looking up at the rocks which seemed to dance around him like a witches coven in their ritual circle. His befuddled mind could almost hear their mad cackling at his misfortune as the toxins from the plant invaded his blood stream.

Lunamor drifted in and out of consciousness unable to tell the difference between reality and the crazy dreams the poisonous plants caused him to suffer. In his head, he heard the impatient voice of Kuu telling him to get up and get himself off to his studies. He thought he heard the Perpetuates whispering to themselves but was only able to make out the occasional word; prophecy, secrets, crystal, danger, Eternal Child, saviour. He was almost sure he felt Rendal place his small bundle under his head to protect it against the hard rocks he laid upon. Strangest of all, he was certain he saw a tall, long-haired Eternal Child bending over him and placing a drinking pouch to his lips encouraging him to drink deeply of a sticky sweet liquid.

When Lunamor groggily came to, the first thing he became aware of was the quality of the lighting. When he had eaten the plant which had caused him to hallucinate it had been mid-morning but he could tell that it was now only just past sunrise. This meant that he had lain here, exposed and vulnerable, for at least one night. Lunamor sat up and brushed off the fog of white fur which had enveloped him whilst he lay dazed. He contemplated the danger he could have been in. Frione had warned him of the dangers of Toku but stupidly he had only been on the lookout for beasts which might cause him harm. This had caused him to be careless of other dangers such as eating plants which were unfamiliar to him. The things that had almost killed him so far were not dangers he had expected; first his near drowning and now poisoning caused by the toxins in strange plants.

Unconsciously, Lunamor put his hand to his lips and realised that they still held the sweet stickiness of the drink he had been offered. Had the Eternal Child who visited him been real? If so, why had he not stayed? Anxious to be on his way, Lunamor pushed himself, unsteadily, to his feet and continued his journey with the uneasy feeling that he had not been alone whilst he slept.

Chapter 20

He had been walking for many hours when an ache in his thighs drew Lunamor's attention to the fact that the ground he walked was beginning to slope slightly upwards. He also noticed that the formations of stone around him were no longer towering as far above his head as they had done previously. Through rocks which were now much more widely spaced, Lunamor was able to occasionally glimpse the glorious blue sky and puffs of white cloud beyond. He was relieved to see that the storm was finally over and breathed in the dust free air beyond the confines of the stone prison he had spent days travelling through.

Before he knew what had happened, he had stepped out from between the final ring of stones and was free of the labyrinth which was Toku. There before him were the foothills of the red stoned mountains of Kriolk. Lunamor gazed up in wonder. Thick swathes of cloud clung to the mountain side so that all that Lunamor could really see was the immense base of the mountain. A narrow dirt trail, bordered by a few enormous trees, led directly from where Lunamor stood. It meandered around a heaped pile of grey boulders and then up to the base of the mountain. Lunamor's eyes continued to follow the curvature of the path as it then began to curl around and around the mountain, backwards and forwards. Clinging precariously to the steep sides of Kriolk were hardy trees in which Lunamor could see bird's nests so huge that he shuddered to think how big the birds must be that had built them.

Lunamor was so overawed by the sheer size of Kriolk, and by the challenge this now posed for him, that he didn't at first notice the complete absence of any noise or signs of life. The constant roar of the winds he had endured during his trek through Toku were now strangely absent and all was still. No insects scuttled, no birds soared through the sky and, if it hadn't been for the swirling mass of cloud surrounding the mountain, Lunamor would have jumped to the conclusion that the world had been frozen in time.

As Lunamor stood hesitantly at the edge of Toku, he became aware of a low rumbling sound far to his left. He felt as though he should know what this sound was but before he had time to consider what might be the cause of it he caught sight of movement out of the corner of his eye. Lunamor quickly turned his head, hoping to catch whatever it was that moved. Nothing. Lunamor scanned the foot of the mountains searching for further signs of anything stirring. He took a few hesitant steps forward. Still nothing.

He made his way along the mud path before him until he found himself shielded from the suns' rays by the leafy branches of a giant banbol tree. At the end of the dirty track, Lunamor could see the huge grey boulders which must have been washed here many millions of moons ago as they were clearly not of the same rusty red rock as the mountains of Kriolk. With the trees blocking out the sunlight and the grey stones blocking the path in front, Lunamor suddenly had the overwhelming feeling of being trapped. There was a feeling of menace in the air and he felt as though he was being forced along this path by some powerful and terrible unseen hand. As though all freewill had left him, Lunamor continued hesitantly down the trail.

Twang! Lunamor's feet shot out from underneath him and, with a scream, he found himself hanging upside down. Both of his feet were secured with some kind of twisted vine which had been bound to the overhanging branches of the trees above him. Having dropped his spear as he was catapulted into the air, Lunamor thrashed his arms around wildly, twisting and turning this way and that in order to try to see what or who had set this trap he now found himself in. Finally, realising that he was completely trapped, Lunamor hung helplessly and awaited whatever was to become of him.

Chapter 21

Suspended in the air, Lunamor's body spun in lazy circles as a gentle breeze caused the branches of the tree he was hanging from to sway. Other than the susurration of the leaves and the creaking of the branch which held his weight, Lunamor could hear no other sound. Just when he thought he was destined to hang here until he passed away from dehydration, Lunamor heard it; an incredibly loud groaning sound as though two plates of rock were being rubbed together and were being placed under immense pressure; a creaking of stiff joints being slowly moved; a sigh of relief, like a grit filled wind, as aching limbs were relieved of their cramped position. The sounds appeared to be coming from behind him and, as Lunamor spun in a slow revolution, the grey boulders he had seen at the end of the trail came into view.

Lunamor realised, with dawning horror, that he had been mistaken. These were not chunks of inanimate rock laying harmlessly at the foot of the mountain but were, in fact, the race of the Toihora. Having straightened out from the tight, ball-like shapes they had used to camouflage themselves, they now stood before him; a group of five huge troll-like creatures. Their skin was the dark grey of gabbro, a rock which consists of interlocking crystals, and was mottled with darker veins which replicated the appearance of the minerals found in this rock. Lunamor noticed that their skin was cragged and rough and had the texture of stone; he was sure that if he were unfortunate enough to rub against it, its coarseness would scrape away his much softer skin.

With a deafening, grating sound, the Toihora moved as one and reached behind themselves for the array of weapons they had hidden there. They brandished these in front of them with a glint of menace in their evil eyes; hatchets which had been sharpened so that the blades were so fine they were almost transparent; bludgeons studded with lethal looking spikes and even a catapult with ammunition made from rocks so large they were bigger than Lunamor's head. As he gazed upon this formidable army, he felt a tremor of fear beginning to shake his whole body.

Their limbs creaking, groaning and rumbling, the Toihora took slow, steady steps towards where Lunamor hung suspended. When they stood, mere moonstones away from where he dangled, they stopped. Lunamor craned his neck in order to be able to peer up into the face of the nearest Toihora. He was just going to begin to unashamedly beg for his life when the features of the Toihora standing closest to him began to ripple from one emotion to another. Lunamor cringed away in terror as the Toihora raised his bludgeon and pointed it towards Lunamor's head. He was sure this was going to be the end and that the Toihora intended to beat him to death but instead the lead Toihora stepped to one side so that his companions could get a closer look at the Eternal Child who hung weakly before them.

In unison, they emitted a gasp like the sound of an avalanche of rocks sliding down a mountainside. Lunamor didn't know what to think but it was clear that for some reason the Toihora were not as sure of their prey as they were previously. The lead Toihora pointed again and Lunamor strained his head to try to see what it was the Toihora were looking at. It was then that he realised that his tunic had come unbuttoned and that the symbol which decorated the side of his neck was now on display for all to see. Before he knew what was happening, one of the Toihora stepped forward and swung his hatchet wide. Lunamor flinched, expecting to feel the sharp sting of the blade at any moment, but instead found himself plummeting to the ground where he landed in a crumpled heap.

He was scooped roughly from the floor by one of the Toihora. His arms restrained by his sides and the craggy surface of the chest of the Toihora rubbing the skin raw at his back, Lunamor struggled fiercely. As he kicked out, his toes made contact with some unseen part of the Toihora's body and a bolt of pain shot up his leg like lightning. Lunamor realised that it was futile to try to escape from the arms that held him when those arms were as solid as rock. The five Toihora pounded along the track, the only sound being the grating and grinding of their great limbs as they moved.. Then, as though they had communicated through telepathy, they turned eastward and marched away from the dirt path they had been following.

The sound of the Toihora as they stomped across the grass at the foot of the mountains of Kriolk was almost deafening. Lunamor's ears rang with the cacophony caused by their moving limbs which was as though a violent earthquake had caused all the mountains of the world to tumble in one go. Despite this noise, he was still able to make out the rumbling sound he had initially heard as he left the confines of Toku. With a growing sense of dread, it suddenly dawned on Lunamor what the cause of the roaring rumble was. A river. The longest and widest river in Orokuvar. A river that ran from south to north along the eastern border. It was a smaller branch of this river that ran underground through the city of Caamond and provided the much needed water to grow crops and to hydrate the city's citizens.

As the small party crested a slight rise in the ground, the river came into view. Its waters poured past in their reckless race to reach the southernmost tip of the land where they would plunge away into nothingness. The river was wide, so wide in fact, that it would have been impossible to bridge it and, even from his slightly elevated position in the Toihora's arms, Lunamor was unable to see the far side. The surface of the river was dotted with lethal looking crops of rocks which jutted out darkly against the vibrant blue of the waters. The Toihora continued to approach the river and then, in unison, stopped.

Lunamor's panic increased. Surely they didn't intend to try to cross this river? Yes, they may be solid and immovable but even the Toihora would not be able to cross the river successfully. They would sink to the bottom of its unknown depths and take him with them. His lungs would fill with the cool waters and would force from him his last desperate breaths. He would never be found again, his body permanently trapped within the arms of the Toihora as he became food for the giant fish that swam within its fathomless depths.

Lunamor searched desperately for the right words to use to plead with the Toihora. Maybe he should offer them the geode which he could feel digging, reassuringly, into his chest due to the pressure of the Toihora's arms wrapped around him. Maybe he should tell them he was the Crystal Bearer. Would they care? Would it make any difference to this race who were incapable of any tender emotion? He began to babble incoherently and it was for this reason that, as the Toihora heaved him into the river, he ingested a large volume of water. As his head rose to the surface, he was just able to make out the rapidly disappearing hulks of the Toihora as they stood and watched him being washed downriver.

Chapter 22

The only water available to the Eternal Children within the walls of Caamond is the river that Lunamor now found himself swept along by. The tributary travels far underground, under the city, and the only way it is reached by the Eternal Children is by the wells they have dug in order to be able to draw the water up to the surface. Within the city walls, there are no lakes, ponds or rivers and so it is for this reason that Lunamor now found himself unable to swim and in grave danger. Swimming wasn't a pastime engaged in by the Eternal Children. Other than his weekly bath, Lunamor had never been fully immersed in water in this way. He certainly had never felt the force of a current such as this which dragged powerfully at anything in its way. The current was caused by the slight downward tilt, from south to north, of the world of Orokuvar. This caused the waters to flow, at great speed, towards the northern brink.

As he was swept along, Lunamor was repeatedly pulled under the water and, in his panicked state, it felt like hours before he was thrown back up to the surface to catch his breath. It was luck that allowed these occasional gasps of sweet air and nothing at all to do with any kind of natural swimming ability Lunamor may have possessed. As he was sped along by the torrents of water, Lunamor tried in vain to grab at any clusters of rocks which came within reach but their surfaces had been worn so smooth over many moons of constant rushing water that he was unable to get any purchase on their slippery facades. Lunamor felt himself being pulled downwards again and, with the last reserves of energy he had, he was able to throw his arm over a large branch of a Kasha tree which was bobbing along beside him in the rapids of the river.

Lunamor coughed and sputtered as he clung to the buoyant branch which was just large enough to support his weight and hold him above the icy depths of the river. His grey curls were pasted across his eyes and he brushed his face against his arm to clear his vision. The western bank of the river was now a long way from where he floated and, as Lunamor twisted to see behind him, he noticed that he was now much closer to the eastern embankment. Both sides of the river were bound by steep banks which would be almost impossible for him to pull himself up on to. Alongside the river, were drooping branches of the tibot trees. The bright white bark of the narrow branches reached out over the river to trail their creamy ivory leaves in the water as though offering to pull Lunamor from the river's grasp.

Now that Lunamor was no longer in immediate danger of drowning, he considered his fate and how he was going to save himself from this plight. He thought back to his Ancient Studies lessons where, as a youngster, he was taught the little geographical knowledge the Eternal Children had of Orokuvar. With the knowledge Lunamor had gathered since leaving the city, he now realised that what he had been taught did not make sense. He had learnt about the river's tributary which flowed deep under the city but the tutors had never gone as far as to say where this had originated from or even where it flowed. It had never occurred to him, at the time, to ask questions of his tutors as this was not something which was encouraged. Even as he was swept along, he had time to wonder where the river's source was. It couldn't be the mountains of Kriolk as he was sure he would have seen the sparkle of the water as it made its way down the mountainside. He couldn't begin to imagine how the river could possibly be formed at the southern edge of Orokuvar.

With a sudden sense of dread, he recalled one particular lesson where the tutors had talked of the boundaries of Orokuvar. He remembered listening, in awe, as he was told of the fact that their world was flat and dropped off into nothingness on all sides. He cursed himself for his stupidity, now, in not asking what would happen to the river and its tributaries as they reached Orokuvar's edge. He also wondered how it was that the Eternal Children could possibly know any of this if they had never left the city walls. This seemed to Lunamor just another way in which he, and the other citizens of Caamond, had been kept in the dark. It was clear to him now that there were those within Caamond who did know more than they were willing to share. What did they have to fear by empowering the race of Eternal Children with knowledge of the world beyond their walls? Not for the first time since he had been exiled, his thoughts turned back to the Perpetuates and added to his growing doubts about their motives for behaving in the way they did.

In his mind, Lunamor pictured the brink of Orokuvar where the Wind Sweepers lived. He recalled the ways in which the Wind Sweepers dove over the edge into the blackness beyond and then used their powerful wings to soar and glide before bringing themselves back to the safety of land. But now Lunamor was helpless; he was being swept along in the fast flowing water and what would happen when he reached the brink? Would there be some kind of invisible barrier to stop the waters or, as he most feared, would there only be empty black space into which the waters would drop, carrying him with them?

Lunamor dragged his body further up onto the branch so that most of his upper body was clear of the water. The constant swirling of the currents meant that the branch twisted and twirled and, as Lunamor was turned dizzily to face the eastern bank, he noticed that there was a stretch of pebbled shore against which the water lapped. Thinking quickly, Lunamor realised that, if he was to escape the powerful torrent of water, he would need to find a way onto that beach. He began to kick his legs, scissoring them rapidly so that he was able to push ahead of him the branch he clung to and fight against the current. Huge waves of water washed over his head as he battled against the river which seemed determined to wash him to oblivion. At one point, he lost his grip on the branch and clutched even harder with his remaining hand. Using all his strength, Lunamor was able to gain a better grip and continued to kick frantically.

Moonstone by moonstone, Lunamor made steady progress towards the beach of rounded pebbles but he could see that not far down river the steep banks returned. If he did not reach the beach soon, he was going to be faced with the insurmountable height of the banks and would be trapped. With renewed vigour and determination, Lunamor kicked more forcefully until he suddenly felt his foot bump against a solid surface. Lunamor let go of the branch and was able to grasp at the jutting rocks and pebbles of the beach and then, panting with exhaustion, he dragged himself up and away from the mighty grasp of the river. He flopped onto his back and lay, gazing up into the diminishing light of the day, catching his breath and thanking his lucky stars for the fact that he had survived.

Chapter 23

The two suns began to sink, lazily, below the horizon and Lunamor shivered; a combination of the fact that he was now soaking wet and the fact that the heat of the day was beginning to dwindle. He sat up and groaned in agony as the movement caused arrows of pain to shoot through his arms and legs which had worked so hard to propel him to the pebbled beach he now lay on. With a feeling of dread, Lunamor felt inside his tunic for the geode but gave a sigh of relief when his hand felt its cool surface. He was also relieved to find the small pouch of Wind Speeder claws still safely confined to his tunic pocket. Unfortunately, the spear he had carried ever since his days spent in the forest of Morupo, had been left behind when he had been captured by the Toihora.

Lunamor slowly got to his feet and then looked around him. In the dying light, he could just make out a cluster of six or seven tibot trees which crowded over the eastern bank of the river. Thinking this might be a good place to shelter for the night, and that it might offer some concealment from any predators that might be on the prowl, Lunamor made his way over to the trees. He entered the small grove of trees and saw that the floor was covered with their ivory leaves. He began to push these together into a pile to make a cushioned bed for the night. As soon as he was satisfied, he sat down on his makeshift bed and struck his Fire Crystal with his knife. Before long he had a comforting blaze in front of him and used its heat to warm his chilled skin and to begin to dry his sodden clothing. His stomach gave a loud growl which could be heard even over the roar of the river and he realised how hungry he was. He still had the leaves of the strange plants of Toku hidden away within his bundle but there was no way he was going to eat these.

Lunamor strolled over to the nearby river bank and threw the leaves into the swirling waters. He watched as they were quickly washed away. He then walked back into the shelter of trees and looked around for something recognisable he might be able to eat. At the furthest edge of the copse, Lunamor spotted a comforting sight, the squat bushes of the bitrob nut. He walked over to the bushes and was delighted to see that the nuts were ripe. The nuts hung in small clusters and were a deep shade of brown so dark that they were almost black. They were about half the size of a moonstone. After a little more exploration, he also discovered the long twisted leaves of the wildress fruit jutting out from amongst the carpet of leaves. He tugged at the leaves and was rewarded with a round scarlet fruit which was also another popular treat of the Eternal Children.

Happy with his find, Lunamor then found a piece of curved bark which he soaked in the rushing waters of the river. He carried his finds over to the fire and placed the nuts and fruit, which he had chopped up, into its bowl-like surface. He then placed the bark into the embers of the fire where the nuts and fruit quickly began to simmer, releasing a glorious aroma. Lunamor sat beside the fire, occasionally giving his fruit and nut stew a gentle stir with a stick and contemplated everything that had happened so far. Somehow he needed to complete his journey south. He was not going to be able to climb Kriolk from the area where the Toihora lived. Their reaction to him had been very strange. It was as though they had recognised the symbol on his neck. Had they seen it before? Why did it cause them such fear? Lunamor also had to consider how he was going to get across to the other side of the river as he now found himself on the wrong side to that on which the mountains of Kriolk were located.

Breaking out of his reverie, Lunamor realised that the bark was beginning to burn and that the nuts and fruit inside were now tender and ready to be eaten. He ate heartily and even licked out the smooth inner surface of the bark afterwards. Once he was satisfied, he threw the piece of bark he had used as a bowl back into the flames and watched as the fire consumed it. He then lay back against his bundle and gazed up into the now dark sky, through the leaves of the tibot tree.

A gentle breeze stirred the branches and Lunamor was able to catch an occasional glimpse of the silver moon. He had travelled far but, somewhere under this same sky, Kuu and the other Eternal Children would be able to see this identical moon. He felt a pang of homesickness as he thought of how it had been growing up with Kuu. His Founder had taught him more than his tutors ever had and he was thankful now for the foraging trips he had accompanied Kuu on. They would often travel to the outskirts of the city, but still within the city walls, and look for wild growing fruits, nuts and vegetables. These weren't skills the tutors thought were useful as all the food the Eternal Children needed was provided by the citizens responsible for farming and distributing food fairly across the city. However, Kuu had enjoyed spending time away from the hustle and bustle of the city and these trips had become something they both enjoyed doing together.

The Eternal Children had no need of survival skills and it was now that Lunamor realised how much of a sheltered existence the Eternal Children lived. They might face little danger in their everyday lives but they also didn't get to experience any great excitement or achievements either. Lunamor had feared for his life whilst in the river but he had survived and this thought made him feel proud. He hoped that, whatever Kuu was doing now, he also felt proud of Lunamor. With the image of his Founder's kindly face in his mind, Lunamor drifted off to sleep.

Chapter 24

Early the next morning, Lunamor began his journey south by following the course of the river. It was a warm day and, welcoming the heat, Lunamor strode happily along the riverbank. He heard birds chirping cheerfully and the constant babbling of the river; the gentle sounds relaxed Lunamor and for the first time he began to enjoy the adventure he was on.

On either side of the river were more of the tibot trees but never more than ten in a cluster; Lunamor was glad that he didn't have to battle his way through another forest. Thoughts of his near miss with the olmflies caused a shiver to travel down his spine. At least here in the open, he could see any dangers that might approach. There was no chance of anything sneaking up on him. When night approached, he made himself another camp and was able to sleep without incident.

Lunamor's journey continued like this for the next two days and he realised how far the river had actually carried him. He could now see the red mountains of Kriolk in the far distance and was heartened to know that his journey had an end in sight. The afternoon of the second day, Lunamor was able to make out a dark shape up ahead but was not able to clearly see what it was. As he drew closer, he realised that a barrier of rocks blocked his way and the only way he would be able to continue was to go around the giant heap. Lunamor was unable to see how far the obstruction stretched for but decided to continue on his way immediately rather than setting up camp for the night.

With the rocks at his right shoulder, Lunamor began to make his way round the barricade and saw that he was now heading into a thicker copse of trees. Every step Lunamor took, carried him further from the bright sunshine and deeper into a tangle of bushes and dense trees. The canopy of trees almost completely blotted out the sky so that Lunamor could only just make out the vague shapes of the strange bushes and trees which crowded in around him. He became aware of a constant dripping sound as water dripped from the ceiling of leaves and branches of the strange trees of the copse. The ground he walked across also felt springy, like a sponge under his feet, and made his journey all the more difficult. As the waterlogged ground sucked at Lunamor's feet, he had to use more and more energy to pull himself free in order to take the next step. Looking behind him, Lunamor realised that he could no longer see the riverbank he had left behind. He also couldn't see very much of what was ahead of him due to the murky quality of the light within what he now realised was a bog.

The ground was now so boggy that Lunamor had to use the trees within arms reach to help pull himself free. He used their sturdy trunks to pull himself forward through the boggy ground. All of a sudden, Lunamor plunged forward into a small clearing within the trees and realised he now had nothing to grab onto to pull himself forward. He was stuck. He tried using both hands to tug himself free until, with a cold finger of dread racing down his spine, he acknowledged the fact that his feet were completely trapped within the sucking, black mud.

Helplessly, Lunamor stopped his futile struggling and looked around him for some way out. The trees bordering the clearing were all out of his reach and there was nothing laying on the clearing floor which he could use to free himself. The light was rapidly waning as day began to turn to evening and it wouldn't be long before Lunamor would be completely trapped in the tar black depths of the bog. He considered shouting for help but quickly dismissed this idea. The last thing he wanted was to alert any nearby Toihora to the fact that he was as helpless as prey caught in a trap. It also wouldn't do to alert any possible dwellers of the bog to the fact that he was completely at their mercy.

Realising that it was down to him and him alone to free himself, Lunamor tried twisting and pulling at his feet but this had the opposite effect to the one he desired. Instead of loosening his feet so that he could pull himself free, he found himself sinking further into the rancid smelling sludge so that he now found himself immersed up to his hips. Lunamor was just beginning to feel all feelings of hope desert him, when the crystal around his neck began to vibrate, emitting a low humming sound as it did so. Glancing down, he noticed that the crystal was radiating its pale lilac light in short pulses as he had seen it do only once before. He scooped the crystal into the palm of his hand and, at his gentle and familiar touch, a bright beam of lilac light shot from its pointed end and pierced the darkness of the bog which surrounded him.

Lunamor moved the beam of light back and forth, picking out strange formations made of a stone-like substance. Eerily, some of these looked almost like Eternal Children with the cragged surfaces taking on the features of the face and the reaching outcroppings looking like grasping hands. Lunamor had the awful thought that maybe he wasn't the first to get trapped in the bog and that, with time, his body would be petrified by the constant water dripping from above thereby providing him with a stony exterior holding him rigidly in place forever. The terrifying through that crossed his mind was that, whilst his body turned to stone, inside he would still be able to think and feel and so he would be suspended in a permanent state of torture.

Lunamor tried to shake off these melancholy thoughts as he continued to drag the beam of light across the darkness ahead of him. He wasn't sure what he was hoping to see but had faith in the power his crystal seemed to provide. He didn't think the crystal would have burst into light at this point for no reason and hoped that this was a sign that help might be on its way in one form or another. Just as Lunamor was considering pointing the beam of light into the air like a beacon in the vain hope of attracting the attention of the Wind Speeder dragons, a sudden movement, like a shadow racing through the trees, caught his eye. Lunamor focused the beam where he had seen the shadows shift and could just make out a dark form far back within the bowels of the bog. The mysterious form was too far back for Lunamor to discern any detail and all he could make out was something which travelled very close to the ground and appeared to be quite wide in stature. Lunamor also noticed that it appeared to be moving stealthily towards him from the shadows.

Without warning, the light of Lunamor's crystal suddenly died away and he was plunged into an all encompassing darkness so black that he felt he could reach out his hand and touch its velvety thickness. Lunamor must have been trapped longer than he had realised as it appeared that day had fully given way to night. As his sense of sight was momentarily stolen from him, all of Lunamor's other senses suddenly seemed to come alive. He could smell the peaty, putrid stench of the rotting boggy waters he was trapped within; he became aware of small insects nipping at his skin to suck the blood from his veins and his hearing was suddenly hyper alert to every sound within the bog. Lunamor could hear the steady hum of the wings of the biting insects, he could hear the soft squelch and slurp of the mud and occasional bubbles of gas popping as they rose to the surface but worst of all, he could hear the slippery sliding noises of the creature which approached him.

Lunamor focused his gaze, intently, on the space where he had last seen the creature moving stealthily towards him. As the noises of the creature drew closer, he began to make out the features of the approaching stranger. The first thing Lunamor was able to see clearly were hugely muscled arms, tinged a faint green colour, which the creature used to drag the rest of its bulk across the mud. Lunamor then noticed that the creature had a broad expanse of chest upon which was draped a very long, plaited beard. This beard grew from the face of a man but as the creature came closer Lunamor could see this was not an Eternal Child but something else entirely. The top half of the body was not much different to that of the Eternal Children, although much more muscular, but the bottom half of the body was that of an eel's tail. It was as shiny and black as obsidian. This was the reason why the creature dragged itself across the mud; using the combined strength of its upper body to pull and the powerful, shiny tail to push and slither its way forward. Without a word the creature grabbed hold of Lunamor's hands in a hold as strong as steel and pulled him from the boggy ground which had held him captive.

Chapter 25

Lunamor lay panting on the slimy ground, partly because of the effort he had exerted in trying to get free and partly in panic at the cold, steely touch of the creature who had pulled him from the sucking mud. Scrabbling desperately, Lunamor pushed himself backwards across the boggy clearing until he was half hidden behind the wide trunk of a tree. The creature, however, gazed at him with a look which was a mixture of concern and amusement. There didn't seem to be any malicious intent in either the way he looked at Lunamor or in the way that he held his body. The creature's arms remained down by his sides and he didn't look as though he was about to pounce, about to attack.

"You needn't be afraid," spoke the creature in a voice which was surprisingly quiet and gentle considering his size, "If I had wanted harm to befall you then I would have left you where you were to satisfy the appetites of the wild beasts of the bog". As he spoke, the creature had moved closer to Lunamor but held out his hands in a calming motion, palms outward to show that he posed no danger. "You must be cold and hungry. My name is Elldrig and my people are called the Amalona. Please, do me the great honour of visiting our home where we will feed you well and where we have many things I am sure you wish to know. It isn't for nothing that you are wandering the perilous bogs alone and your presence here doesn't come as a complete surprise to my race."

As the Amalona spoke, Lunamor felt a warmth spread through him at the calming resonance of Elldrig's voice. The soothing tones had the effect of a heated blanket being spread over his cold shoulders and Lunamor felt all the exertions of the day, and the tension pent up within him, seep out until all the muscles of his body released their coiled energy and relaxed. Holding out his right hand in greeting to Elldrig, Lunamor said, "I'm Lunamor. I've travelled from the city of Caamond and am heading for the mountains of Kriolk."
"I know," stated Elldrig simply and he then motioned for Lunamor to follow him.

As they travelled through the bog, Elldrig explained how he had been out hunting when he had spotted the beam of light from Lunamor's crystal. It was this that had led him to discover Lunamor trapped in the boggy ground. Now that he was being guided by Elldrig, who knew every inch of the bogs, he found that he was able to walk much more easily. The Amalona stuck to almost invisible paths of firmer ground. These wound this way and that way through the closely growing trees but Elldrig moved without hesitation, showing a familiarity born of many years of living in the bogs. The mud no longer sucked at his feet and so Lunamor was able to keep up with Elldrig who slid effortlessly across the damp ground.

Before long, Lunamor found himself standing at the foot of a tree so large he couldn't see any branches, only the great expanse of the trunk of the tree which seemed to go up and up as far as the eye could see. At the bottom of the trunk were a mass of tangled roots which wove in and out of each other haphazardly. Lunamor watched in amazement as Elldrig leant towards the tree and gently rested his forehead against one section of tree root which was wider than his own chest. As soon as Elldrig's flesh came into contact with the roots they seemed to unfurl and unknot themselves until a wide opening had appeared before them. Elldrig straightened and then led Lunamor down, through the roots, and into the underground home of the Amalona.

Lunamor was astonished to see that the tunnel under the tree was well lit by burning branches which jutted from the walls at regular intervals. The tunnel was so broad that he could not have touched either side even with his arms stretched wide. The floor of the tunnel sloped gently downwards and had been worn as smooth as glass by what Lunamor assumed was generations of Amalona and their eel-like tails. It was also noticeably warmer underground and surprisingly inviting.

They didn't seem to have travelled far when the tunnel split into two; the left branch of the tunnel was dark and forbidding but to the right the flaming torches continued to light the way. It was in this direction that Elldrig guided Lunamor. "The tunnel to the left is rarely used," explained Elldrig, "This is why we don't bother to light it. There is something down there that we will wish to show you but now is not the time. First you need to eat, sleep and hear our story; in that order." By now, Lunamor was beginning to feel incredibly weary. He could tell that the Amalona were a peaceful race, just as the Wind Speeders were, and using some deeply buried instinct he knew that, whilst he was sheltered under the roots of their tree, they would do everything in their power to protect him.

"Here we are," declared Elldrig and he led Lunamor into a huge hall which had been hollowed out of the ground. Hanging from the ceiling hung a knot of roots which were ablaze with golden flames. Lunamor's mouth fell open in shock and, as though reading his mind, Elldrig explained, "The roots are coated with oils extracted from the boggy waters and it is these that burn, rather than the roots. We have a system in place which feeds the oils into all parts of the root so that the flames never burn through to the actual wood beneath. This means that we can have this light burning at all times. We use the same method on the torches which light our tunnels."

Lunamor continued to look around in awe. The hall was filled with many more Amalona, some in groups and some sitting alone, who all turned to look at Lunamor as he entered. He should have felt uncomfortable under the scrutiny of so many pairs of eyes, but instead he just felt an overwhelming feeling of calm. It was as though the Amalona exuded an aura of peace and wellbeing which affected everybody around them. It had the effect of making him feel welcome as though he had arrived to visit old friends he spent much time with.

Lunamor watched as Elldrig approached a small cooking fire around which sat three female Amalona. They wore intricately woven shawls wrapped tightly around their chests and tied around the necks and had long flowing curls which tumbled down, ending in the small of their backs just above where their eel-like tails began. Elldrig spoke quietly to one of the three female Amalona and then accepted a small steaming bowl, ladled from what had been cooking in the vast pot hung over the fire. Elldrig turned back to Lunamor and indicated he should follow him down another smaller passage which led off from the hall. This was one of many similar tunnels which dotted the outer edges of the hall.

As he walked through the smaller tunnel, Lunamor noticed that the lights were dimmer here and after a few hundred moonstones distance he began to notice that a series of holes had been hollowed out of the walls on either side. These were filled with feathers of all shape, size and colour and to Lunamor they looked incredibly inviting. Elldrig suddenly stopped at a hollow filled with feathers of all shades of blue and white. The sight reminded Lunamor of the fluffy white clouds which drifted across the sky on a summer's day. "Eat the broth within this bowl and then leave it on the floor beside your sleeping chamber. You need to get some sleep as we have lots to talk about once you feel rested." With that, Elldrig turned and slid back up the tunnel towards the hall.

Lunamor shovelled the delicious broth into his mouth and then placed the bowl on the floor. He then reached up to the lip of the hollow and pulled himself into the sleeping chamber. His body sank into his bed of feathers gratefully and before he was even aware that he had lain down his head he was fast asleep.

Chapter 26

The melodic sound of a bell awoke Lunamor gently from the deep sleep he had fallen into. He had no idea how long he had slept, but his body was well rested and his mind felt alert and ready to learn what he could from what the Amalona had to tell him. Lunamor lowered himself from the sleeping chamber and made his way along the dimly lit passage towards the great hall.

He emerged from the opening of the tunnel into the hall which seemed to serve as the communal space for the tribe of Amalona who lived there. As before, there were groups of Amalona dotted around the hall and in his refreshed state Lunamor now noticed that many of these appeared to be family groups. They were made up of two adult Amalona and then one or two juvenile Amalona. This was very different to the family groups in Lunamor's home city of Caamond where Newlings lived with their Founder and so there were only ever two within the family unit.

He watched with interest as the two adults, sometimes of the same gender or sometimes different, interacted lovingly with each other and their offspring. Gestures of tender affection were shared regularly; a touch of an arm, a pat on the head or the occasional cuddle and Lunamor felt a surge of homesickness as he thought of his Founder Kuu.

Eternal Children didn't share these same types of physical displays of affection however Lunamor could recall the strong bond he shared with Kuu which was demonstrated by an easy companionship, the ability to almost read the other's mind and to know how the other was feeling in any given moment. This was engendered through being in each other's company from the moment of the Founding until the very second the coming of age ceremony was performed. In order for the Newling to develop into a productive and useful citizen of Caamond, the Founder must narrate every action and share every thought so that the Newling knows everything that their Founder knows.

In theory, this worked well in passing along not only knowledge but also a uniform way of thinking and acting. This meant that the Eternal Children of Caamond rarely squabbled, never did anything unexpected and certainly never challenged the things they were told by the Perpetuates. It was clear now that Lunamor was unlike any other Eternal Child and he wondered if that is also why he had been Found by Kuu. Had some mysterious fate ensured that the one Founder the Newling Lunamor ended up with was the only one who would accept and understand his many questions growing up?

Shrugging off his sudden yearning for home, Lunamor spotted Elldrig deep in conversation with an Amalona who seemed to be much older. Threads of dark grey wove through his beard and hair; the slick surface of his tail lacked the lustre of the younger Amalona and his flesh appeared more weathered with deep creases in his forehead and eyes. These creases had the combined effect of making the ancient Amalona appear thoughtful at the same time as merry. Elldrig made eye-contact with Lunamor and gestured, with a wave of his hand, that he should join the pair.

As he approached the duo, the old Amalona opened his arms wide and pulled Lunamor into a warm embrace. Unused to such physical contact with another, Lunamor held himself stiffly at first and then relaxed into the hug. The Amalona gave him a hearty pat on the back and then stepped away. "We have been expecting you these many years but I had started to think that you would not arrive in my lifetime," proclaimed the Amalona.

"This is Aaljum, our tribe leader," explained Elldrig as he smiled a greeting at Lunamor, "He has been waiting many, many moons for you to arrive."

"It's an honour to meet you," said Lunamor who, despite the stories he had already heard on his journey about the prophecy, was surprised when he was greeted with such enthusiasm.

Inside, he didn't really feel any different and he certainly didn't feel as though he was special enough or skilled enough to ensure that a prophecy, such as he had heard tell, would come to pass. It seemed that everybody he came into contact with either went out of their way to help him or else tried to kill him. What did this say about these foes? Had they not heard of the prophecy and therefore had no reason to believe he was important in the way of those who had helped him? Or did they know of the prophecy and were doing everything in their powers to ensure it did not come to pass? The idea that there may be those out there who were willfully going out of their way to destroy him was not a thought that gave him any comfort.

Aaljum indicated that the group should move over to an area where large blankets of a vibrant cyan velvet were draped over mounds of springy hay and together they sat companionably. Lunamor looked at Aaljum expectantly and waited patiently for him to speak. It seemed that the chief Amalona had decided that the best place to start was by explaining some of the history of the Amalona tribe.

Our tribe, the Amalona, rarely leave the boglands now but there was a time, many, many moons ago, when we would travel far across this world to learn all we could from its inhabitants. As a right of passage, any Amalona who were on the verge of stepping into maturity, would venture into new and uncharted territory. The purpose: to bring back new knowledge which would strengthen our tribe.

It is only because of the many brave voyagers who have ventured out into the dangerous unknown that we have been able to map our world and place upon this map the various species which inhabit it. There are few areas of this world that we haven't explored; the only area unknown to us being the mountains of Kriolk.

"When Elldrig explained that you had travelled from the city of Caamond and were heading to the mountains of Kriolk, I knew, as he also did in that moment, that you were the one we have been waiting for; the Crystal Bearer of whom the prophecy speaks. Caamond was one of the first places charted on our maps and we have known, for many generations, that it is inhabited by the Eternal Children. There are some of Orokuvar who do not welcome interaction with outsiders and so we have only been able to observe Caamond from afar. From our observations of the citizen's of Caamond, it's true, you do appear to share many of the same features but, as you are probably already aware, there is another race out there which is very similar. I hope that the tale I have to tell will allow you to continue your journey with hope in your heart." As Aaljum explained all of this he had looked at Lunamor with compassion in his eyes and Lunamor could tell that before him sat a great leader. A leader who cared for those he led, who was incredibly wise and who could be relied upon to do the best he could for those in his care.

"This is certainly what has troubled me most since being exiled from Caamond," declared Lunamor passionately who still felt the hurt of that moment. It was an ache in his heart as though somebody had reached into the very depths of him and had removed the essence of who he thought he was. He was sure that, if he had an answer to the question of why he was different, of why he was the only one with the strange symbol on his neck and the only one Found with the geode which he knew contained power far greater than anything he had yet been able to unleash, then that pain would begin to ease a little. He would be able to make his peace with the fact that he had never really belonged there and could hopefully continue his expedition knowing that he was journeying towards his true home and not away from it.

"Before I tell you our story, you need to know that I cannot tell you what you are heading towards. We have been unable to explore the mountains of Kriolk because of a long standing feud with the Toihora. An uneasy truce was formed, only when we promised that we would not venture into the mountain region and since that moment we have kept our word," explained Aaljum.

"Maybe it is time we showed Lunamor what our ancestors created so that he is more easily able to understand the story we have to share," suggested Elldrig softly. Aaljum nodded in agreement and, together, he and Ellrdig rose and, without another word, led Lunamor out of the hall and along the tunnel he had travelled the day before.

Chapter 27

Shortly, the three arrived at the entrance to the darkened tunnel Lunamor had seen the previous day. Elldrig took one of the burning branches from its intricately carved sconce of wood to the left hand side of the mouth of the passage. Holding the torch aloft, he led the way with Aaljum and Lunamor following closely behind. Lunamor noticed that the passage slanted downwards ever so slightly and that the ground under his feet was much rougher than the other tunnels he had walked. He figured that this probably meant that this passageway was not travelled down often and so had not been worn smooth by the friction of countless Amalona tails.

The further into the tunnel they walked, the more Lunamor began to feel uneasy. He was unused to such confined spaces and the thought of the weight of rock and soil pressing down above his head caused him a momentary pang of panic. He was just considering asking how much further, when the narrow passage suddenly opened out into a small, rectangular shaped cavern. Lunamor watched in curiosity as Elldrig approached the far wall and began to touch the end of his torch to a series of other torches set along the wall in a straight line just below the height of the low ceiling. As he did so, Lunamor finally saw what it was the Amalona had wanted him to see.

Directly opposite the entrance to the chamber, was a mosaic which covered the entire wall. It was made from shards and slivers of crystal, geode and precious stones, some of which Lunamor was familiar with, and others that were unknown to him. As the torches flared into life above the intricate array of pieces, the flickering flames glinted off of the sparkling shards so that it almost appeared as though the image before him moved.

The mosaic contained so much detail that Lunamor thought it might take him a lifetime to discover the story it illustrated. It was for this reason that Lunamor was relieved when Aaljum began to speak.

"This mosaic was created dozens of generations ago after a group of four Amalona adventurers returned from their travels. The chief at the time felt that what they had to share was so momentous it needed to be recorded in such a way that it would never be forgotten by the Amalona." As he spoke Aaljum had moved towards the mosaic and now indicated an area to the far right which depicted a figure seated with a cluster of Amalona. Lunamor leaned forward to take a closer look and gasped when he saw that the figure Aaljum pointed to was Lunamor's own exact likeness. The same pale grey curls, the smattering of celestial freckles across the cheekbones, the broad muscular back and chest and, most telling of all, the unusual symbol which adorned his neck.

"This is the point at which we find ourselves now," explained Aaljum, "but we shouldn't start at the end. We need to begin at the beginning." The ancient Amalona chief moved over to the far left of the mosaic and pointed to a section which showed four Amalona standing to attention, spears in hand, and watching the approach of what were clearly the same five travellers Rendol had spoken of.

"These were your ancestors, Lunamor, and they told an interesting tale which it is now my honoured duty to share with you."

Aaljum swept his hand slightly to the right to draw Lunamor's attention to the next scene shown in the mosaic. "Your ancestors stopped a mere stone's throw away from our young adventuring Amalona. Clearly sensing the younger Amalonas' nervousness, the five tall voyagers laid down the spears they carried, as well as their other weapons of bows and arrows and knives. Unarmed, they introduced themselves as the Eternal Children of the Kriolk peaks," narrated Aaljum. As he spoke, Lunamor noticed, for the first time, that in the background of this scene, behind the five Eternal Children, were the red mountains of Kriolk, the peaks lost in a haze of cloud.

Without any prompting from Aaljum, Lunamor's gaze continued to the right where he noticed that the Amalona and the Eternal Children were now illustrated as sitting around a huge campfire. He felt in awe at the incredible skill used to show the fiery glow of the flames which had been created using broken splinters of amber, ruby shards and flakes of citrine. But what caught his attention most were the scattering of tiny diamonds which had been inlaid into a background of the blackest onyx Lunamor had ever seen. Lunamor didn't need Aaljum to explain to him that this was the shower of stars that his ancestors had followed across the world.

"I can see from your face that you are already aware of the stars which fell from the heavens but there is still more for you to learn. Your ancestors explained that they followed this shower of stars because of a prediction which I'm sure you now know is more prophecy than prediction. What you may not know is that this shower of stars was going to deliver to this world the one who would fulfil this prophecy, one who was of the same race as the Eternal Children of the Kriolk peaks. It was for this reason that these travellers now followed these stars. They hoped to retrieve the geode, carried within the downpour of stars, and thereby bring home the Crystal Bearer to his own people," explained Aaljum.

"But I don't understand," declared Lunamor, "The final scene here shows myself being greeted by you, the Amalona. When we first met, you were not surprised to learn that I came from Caamond. How can it be that, if my ancestors came in search of me, I was raised in Caamond?"

"Something clearly went wrong." announced Aaljum. "Before your ancestors continued their journey, they agreed to pass through our bogs on their return home. My forefathers waited for many moons but your people never appeared. Instead, we were visited by a Tugarl."

"I have heard of the prophecy carried by the Tugarl," declared Lunamor. "What more did he have to say of what had happened to my people?"

"I'm afraid it is not good news, Lunamor," stated Aaljum sadly. "I will share with you what happened when the Tugarl placed his hand on the forehead of the chief at the time.

At his touch, a scene was played out in the Amalona chief's mind. He watched as the Eternal Children of the Kriolk peaks approached the point where the showers of stars rained down to meet the earth. The twinkling pinpricks were many and the five travellers continued forward into the astral monsoon; sparks bouncing off their shoulders, broad backs and exposed heads. Then, suddenly, there was a blinding light and the five voyagers seemed to have disappeared and in their place, stood the city walls of Caamond, proud and tall.

"That was all my chief saw but it was enough for him to know that the Eternal Children of the Kriolk peaks would not be returning. It appeared that they had failed in their mission but the prophecy still stood. Despite the fact that they had been unable to bring you home to your people, here you are," finished Aaljum.

Completely overwhelmed by everything he had heard, Lunamor sank to the floor of the chamber with his head in his hands. Elldrig and Aaljum looked on, with sympathy in their eyes, before finally turning away and leaving Lunamor to grieve for the ancestors he had never known.

Chapter 28

When Lunamor finally became aware of his surroundings, he had no idea how long he had remained crouched alone in the dark. His muscles felt stiff and goosebumps covered his flesh from the cold damp air of the chamber. Lunamor rose to his feet and, taking one last, lingering look at the incredible mosaic of the Amalona, he then turned and made his way back down the seldom used tunnel and back to the main hall.

Silently, Lunamor emerged into the communal living space of the Amalona. As before, he was overcome by the sense of community within the Amalona people. Over a large fire, hung a huge metal pot, inside which, bubbled a delicious smelling stew. Lunamor's mouth watered and he realised, with a griping pain in his stomach, how hungry he was. The day's events had drained him and he now felt the need to re-energise.

Elldrig approached and clasped Luanamor's cold hands warmly between his own. He drew Lunamor further into the room and indicated that the Eternal Child should take a seat on the cushioned benches that circled the cooking fire. Welcoming the heat, Lunamor felt the tension leach from his body. In twos and threes, more and more of the Amalona joined Elldrig and Lunamor around the fire until everyone was seated.

As though reacting to a signal that only they could hear, the Amalona turned their faces towards the opening of a tunnel which was to the right of the immense fire they had gathered around. This was a tunnel that Lunamor had not noticed before and he realised this was because its entrance had previously been covered by a thick, black curtain of a velvety material which had now been drawn to one side to reveal the opening behind it. The opening of the tunnel was flanked, on either side, by tapestries woven from a material which was unidentifiable to Lunamor. The fine fibres had been knitted together to create wall hangings of unimaginable detail.

The tapestry to the left of the tunnel portrayed Orokuvar in its infancy. Streams were a mere trickle as they flowed from the mountains of Kriolk which were much higher in the world's beginning. The trees of Morupo were slender saplings, yet to grow into the densely growing forest of giants that Lunamor had journeyed through. Lunamor's eyes were drawn to the empty space of land where his home, Caamond, should have been located but, in the early days of this world, Caamond was not yet a reality. Beyond the eleven edges which marked the boundary of the land, was shown the deep black of nothingness speckled with the now familiar spattering of silver stars.

In contrast, the tapestry to the right of the opening depicted a much more disturbing scene. Lunamor could now see the mature trees of the forest of Morupo and he could see the great river along which he had walked only a few short days ago. He could also see the mountains of Kriolk and, at their foot, the rocky paths of Toku which, on the first tapestry were a solid expanse of rock, but on this second image showed the narrow passages carved from the stone by thousands of moons of exposure to the elements. It wasn't this now familiar landscape which had so distressed Lunamor but the intricately embroidered images of fearsome beasts which soared and prowled the skies above the land. They appeared to writhe in agony amongst a backdrop of threatening and pendulous clouds which boiled and bubbled over the vista below.

As Lunamor studied the tapestries, he became aware of the fact that the tunnel in between these wall hangings was slowly becoming lighter. Aaljum emerged from the tunnel carrying, in his right hand, a single candle set in a pewter coloured candle-holder. In the other hand, the chief of the Amalona tribe carried a small object which was not much bigger than the palm of his hand. The object was wrapped in a fragment of material which had once had a golden sheen but had now faded to a dull and dingy beige. It was tied around with a length of waxed twine and the knot on top had been sealed with a scarlet wax seal.

Aaljum made his way across the great hall and stopped a few paces away from where Lunamor sat. Lunamor was unable to read the expression which flickered across Aaljum's face; it seemed to be a mixture of sympathy, awe and even a little bit of fear. "I didn't tell you everything whilst we were in the tunnels," explained Aaljum, "There is one more thing you need to know. Before your ancestors departed they left an item with us for safekeeping. This item was, and still is, of great importance to your people. They placed their greatest trust in us when they left this item and they asked that we keep it until they returned. As you know, they never came back. This item now belongs to you. It needs to be returned to your people." As he finished speaking, Aaljum held the bundle out towards Aaljum. The eyes of all the gathered Amalona followed the package as it was transferred from Aaljum's hands and into Lunamor's trembling grasp.

The package was much heavier than Lunamor had expected considering its small size. Through the material, Lunamor was able to feel that the object inside was of a very similar shape to his geode but far, far heavier. Now that he was able to see the package up close he noticed that the ruby wax seal had had a symbol pressed into it; it was the same symbol which adorned Lunamor's neck. With clumsy fingers, Lunamor peeled away the seal and tugged at the knot which held the package closed. As he finally loosened the knot, the pieces of material wrapped around the package fell open and revealed the most wondrous sight.

In his hands, Lunamor held a fragment of pallasite. From his lessons in Caamond, Lunamor recognised this for what it was. Lunamor knew, from his studies, that pallasites were extremely rare and he had never seen an actual example of one. In fact, he didn't know of any other Eternal Child that had seen one, not even the Perpetuates. The pallasite he now held in his hands was flat in shape, almost as though it had been shaved from a larger chunk of meteorite, and was polished to a high shine. As he held it out in front of him, the glow from the fire caused the golden specks which decorated its surface to glitter. It was then that Lunamor noticed that there was some type of writing on the surface facing away from him which stood out against the otherwise slightly opaque surface. Lunamor turned the piece of pallasite over and almost dropped it when he read the words that had been carved into its surface.

Peril sees this world defiled,
By creatures, dangerous and wild,
For all to be reconciled,
Search the stars for the Exiled Child.

The words of the prophecy etched on the surface of the pallasite brought to Lunamor's mind the wall hanging which hung behind Aaljum. Once again, his eyes explored the embroidery and took in the hideous creatures that haunted the skies. Noticing where Lunamor's gaze had travelled, Aaljum spoke, "This embroidery was created after your ancestors had left. They had shared with us the words written on the object you now hold. Neither us nor them know of what dangers the prophecy speaks but my ancestors allowed their imaginations to run amok."

"How did this pallasite come to be in the possession of my people?" asked Lunamor. "Your ancestors described a shower of rocks falling from the heavens. Trails of fire blazed across the sky and, from their position high up in the Kriolk mountains, they watched as the land below was hit with a hail of rocks. The last to fall was this pallasite which hit the peak of the mountains. Fortunately, none of the Eternal Children was harmed. When they had gathered the courage to investigate, they found this pallasite you now hold and with the message it contained engraved for all to read." Aaljum looked to Elldrig as he spoke and a silent message seemed to pass between the two. "You have learnt a lot today and I'm sure that you have a lot to think about," stated Elldrig, "I think that you will be wanting to continue your journey shortly so you must eat and then rest."

Lunamor nodded distractedly and allowed Elldrig to press a bowl of delicious smelling stew into his hands. As though in a trance, Lunamor ate and then rose, without a word, and returned to the chamber he had slept in the previous night. Lunamor didn't think there was any chance he would sleep after the events of the day but, with the geode and the pallasite both safely tucked into his tunic pocket, he quickly fell asleep.

Chapter 29

Lunamor had no idea how long he had slept when he was awoken by the subdued murmur of voices and gentle weeping. Most of the tunnel was in darkness but Lunamor could see a light flickering faintly a short way further down the tunnel from the hollow he slept in. Curious, Lunamor extricated himself from the nest of feathers and lowered himself to the tunnel floor. He made his way cautiously towards the light, unsure of what he was going to find. He was also mindful of the fact that his presence may not be welcomed there. After all, he was a stranger to the Amalona.

It wasn't long before Lunamor arrived at the source of the light to discover a small group of Amalon gathered soberly at the opening to one of the sleeping hollows. Nestled in amongst the feathers was a male Amalona. His hair and beard, which were streaked with thick stripes of white and grey, surrounded a face that was creased up with pain. Unlike the other males of his species, his upper torso was skeletal. Stick thin arms lay folded across his chest which rose and fell jerkily as he desperately sucked in air. With each exhalation a ghastly rattle could be heard and Lunamor winced in sympathy.

Suddenly, Lunamor became aware of a presence behind him and looked over his shoulder to see Elldrig standing behind him. "He's dying," sighed Elldrig, "There's nothing we can do to help him. We have seen this strange sickness before but it was a long, long time ago. The last time we saw it, it spread through the tribe and wiped out many of our older members."
"But isn't there a cure?" asked Lunamor, "Surely you must have medicines!"
"The last time the sickness spread, we had almost given up hope of any of us surviving but then the Tugarl arrived and brought with him the only cure that could stop the terrible sickness before it wiped us out completely," explained Elldrig, "There is no place the Tugarl cannot go. He knows all, sees all and is welcome to all. This is why he was able to spend time with the Wind Speeder dragons and, before leaving them, was gifted with their most precious gift; their claws. The Tugarl has power greater than that we could ever know and, not only does he know everything that has come to pass, he also seems to know everything that is yet to be. It seems that, after leaving the Wind Speeder dragons he travelled straight to us, where we awaited in dire need of a cure to heal our sick and dying. Unfortunately, we have no more of that medicine left. It is too late for this Amalona. Even if we send a new party of Amalona in search of the Tugarl, the chances of us ever finding one are very slim."

Suddenly Lunamor's face lit up with excitement as he remembered the gift passed to him by the Wind Speeder dragons. Lunamor quickly hurried back to the hollow where, not so long ago, he had been fast asleep. He pulled out his small bundle and dug around in the jumbled contents until his fingers felt the silky smooth surface of the pouch. He pulled it out and handed the bag, triumphantly, to Elldrig. A look of recognition flitted across the Amalon's face and, with trembling fingers, he pulled open the drawstring bag to reveal the shimmering claws of the Wind Speeders. "How did you get these? No it doesn't matter, there is no time for that now."

Lunamor watched as Elldrig slithered up the tunnel in great haste and was swallowed up by the darkness of the tunnel. In no time at all he was back and this time Aaljum followed closely behind. In Alljum's cupped hands, was a quartz pestle and mortar. Lunamor watched curiously as Aaljum tipped one of the dragon claws into the pestle and began to carefully grind the claw into a fine powder. When the chief was happy with the consistency of the powder, he approached the deathly pale Amalona. Aaljum took a pinch of the powder between thumb and forefinger and held it to the nostril of the Amalona who lay desperately ill. The powder was swiftly inhaled up the Amalona's nose.

Those stood around the hollow held their breath and, before their very eyes, they watched as the colour returned to the cheeks of the ill Amalona male. Lunamor was amazed to see muscle building on the arms and chest, even as he watched. The Amalona's beard and hair became thick and lustrous and turned a glossy black. His eyes flickered open and the previously ill Amalona looked around him in surprise; a look of utter bewilderment washed across his face and he was smothered by the embraces of his loved ones.

Feeling like an intruder, Lunamor slowly backed away from the happy scene. Who was there to care if he became sick or died? Who would rejoice if he were to overcome great illness just as this Amalona had? Despite the fact that he knew more now than he ever had about his ancestors, he still didn't feel as though he had anyone he could call family. Even Kuu was becoming a long distant memory which was becoming more hazy the further Lunamor travelled away from Caamond. His last thoughts, before he fell back asleep, were of the intense desire to be welcomed into a family of his own.

Chapter 30

The next morning, Lunamor sought out Elldrig and requested that he be taken to speak to Aaljum. Elldrig led the way across the huge, central caverns and over to the tunnel flanked on either side by the tapestries Lunamor had studied the day before. The thick curtain was drawn closed across the opening and Elldrig reached up to a tasselled pull cord to the left. With a gentle tug the curtain was swept, swiftly, to the side to reveal the tunnel behind.

As with the tunnel leading to the mosaic, this tunnel was not worn as smooth as the tunnel to the sleeping chambers. Unlike the chamber leading to the mosaic, this tunnel did not slant downwards and was well lit. Before long the tunnel widened out into a surprisingly cosy cave carved out of the rock. A small fire burned in a fireplace which had been chiselled out of the stone and the fragrant aroma of burning wood filled the room. To the side of the fireplace was a tall backed wooden chair. The chair looked to have been whittled out of one solid piece of wood. Lunamor noticed the whorls and knots in the wooden surface which had been sanded down to a silky smoothness. The whole thing then appeared to have been varnished with some kind of shiny liquid which gave the chair a highly polished appearance. To make the chair more comfortable, piles of cushions had been heaped onto its wide seat and it was here that Aaljum was seated.

"Ah, Lunamor! I had thought that, after the excitement last night, you might have slept late today but I am sure I know the reason why you stand here now before me. You are ready to continue your journey, are you not?" asked Aaljum.
"Yes," stated Lunamor simply. There seemed to be so much more he needed to say. Dozens of questions seemed stuck at the back of his throat. He wanted to squeeze them out past his lips and hear the answers that Aaljum had to give but he knew that this wasn't the way it needed to be done. In fact, he wasn't even sure that Aaljum would have any answers to give. Could the chief of the Amalona know how he, Lunamor, had come to be found outside the city gates of Caamond? Could he know why the Tugarl had not yet sought out Lunamor himself in order to share the answers he surely held? And it was surely impossible that Aaljum would know what awaited him when he finally reached the peaks of Kriolk. This was Lunamor's biggest fear. That when he finally arrived at the summit of Kriolk there would be nobody there. Or worse still, that those who were there would want nothing to do with him.

"We thank you most graciously for the gift of those Wind Speeder claws. Without them, our beloved one would not have survived," added Aaljum.
"It is I who should be thanking you," protested Lunamor. "If it was not for Elldrig I would have sunk, in despair, into the boggy ground. If it had not been for your ancestors I would not have heard what the Tugarl and my own people had to say. And were it not for you and the leaders before your time I would not have the pallasite in my possession. I owe you more than words can say. You must keep the rest of the claws," insisted Lunamor and he held the pouch out towards Aaljum.

Aaljum took the silken pouch gratefully and gave a thoughtful nod to himself. "Yes, you are the Crystal Bearer, I am in no doubt about that. I know that when you leave here this will not be the last we hear of you. I know that, whatever dangers our world faces, you are the one who will be our saviour. Take care on your journey. Elldrig will escort you to the edges of the bog to ensure that you are able to leave our lands safely."

With that, Elldrig began to lead the way back up the tunnel. He didn't stop at the main cavern but continued up the tunnel Lunamor had followed him down just two short days ago but which now felt like a lifetime. Gradually the floor began to slope upwards and, before long, Elldrig leant forward and touched his forehead to what appeared to be a solid wall in front of him. As before, the wall seemed to uncurl itself, revealing a mass of tree roots, and then Lunamor and Elldrig were once again standing in the murky air of the boglands.

Elldrig began to lead the way with the easy familiarity of someone who has travelled through the area many times before. He wound in and out of the trees that were dotted in their path and Lunamor made sure to step exactly where Elldrig's tail passed. The last thing he wanted was to find himself sinking into the stagnant mud again. It took much less time than he had thought it would and ,after only a few hours, they had reached the edge of the Amalonas' land.

Lunamor and Elldrig had not spoken much as they journeyed through the bogs. Mainly because it seemed that everything that needed to be said had already been spoken but also because there was now an easy companionship between them. In the short time they had known each other, they had developed a feeling of mutual respect and admiration. This was not the relationship of a rescuer and the rescued or even of the Crystal Bearer and his aid. This was the beginning of a real and life-long friendship. Despite the fact that Elldrig and Lunamor had not, in fact, spent so very long in conversation they both saw in each other very similar traits. Like recognises, and seeks, like. Lunamor was sure that, in the future, his path would cross Elldrig's again.

Lunamor peered past the boundary of the bogs and was relieved to see the two suns shining high in the sky. He allowed Elldrig to clasp him, briefly, to his chest and then patted Elldrig on the arm before turning his back on the Amalona and continuing his journey southwards.

Chapter 31

After being confined to the murky bogs, and then the underground home of the
Amalona for so long, the sunshine felt glorious on his skin. He could feel the
powerful rays beating down on him and welcomed them. To his right, he could hear
the gentle roar of the river and altered his course so that he was moving in a
south-westerly direction. This meant that he was moving closer to the Kriolk
mountains but also closer to the river which he desperately needed to cross.

Lunamor didn't relish the thought of having to enter the river's powerful depths again.
He cursed himself for not mentioning this to Elldrig and Aaljum as he was sure they
would have been able to give him some idea as to how he was going to cross the
river. With a sigh, he put this concern out of his mind for the moment and began to
take in a little more of his surroundings.

He found that he was walking across open grassland which was speckled with a
colourful array of flowers. The land was flat to the east and west and, when he
looked back, he could just make out the receding treeline of the boglands. Before he
had encountered the Toihora, he had almost reached the foot of the Kriolk mountains
and he could still see their formidable bulk in front of him in the direction he travelled.
In order to reach the mountains though, he was going to need to cross the river. He
knew that the river couldn't be too far away and so he picked up his pace a little,
determined to reach the river before nightfall.

It was as he stopped to take a rest that Lunamor suddenly became aware of a slight
vibration which seemed to be coming through the ground and travelling up his legs.
Looking down, he noticed that small pebbles were bouncing crazily as the vibrations
caused shockwaves through the earth. Alarmed, Lunamor shaded his eyes from the
suns and looked around in all directions. He had the terrifying thought that he might
be about to run into the Toihora again. Weirdly though, he couldn't see anything
threatening and so he continued cautiously on his way.

The land had begun to steadily climb in a gentle slope and Lunamor could feel a
slight ache in his calves as he walked up the incline at a rapid pace. As he reached
the height of the incline he was faced with the cause of the vibrations he had been
feeling. There before him were the Kriolk mountains he had travelled so far to reach.
True, they were on the wrong side of the river but he could see now how he would be
able to get to the western bank.

The magnificent pink tones of the rocky mountains glowed in the dusky light of the
setting suns. The suns had now begun their descent and, as they did so, their rays
shifted through uncountable shades of pink, red and purple before they would sink
completely out of sight and leave the world in darkness. Now the glorious rays of the
sun combined with the pinky tones of the mountain to create a spectacular scene
before Lunamor. This was made all the more magical because of the fact that a jet
of water was shooting from the centre of the mountain, about half way up. This jet of
water spurted high into the air like the arc of a bridge and then fell back to the land
again to create the beginnings of the river. As the water hit land, it caused powerful

shock waves to travel through the ground. At least Lunamor now knew the source of the river, if not where it ended.

Lunamor stood mesmerised. He was overwhelmed by the sheer beauty of what he saw. Droplets of water sparkled in the evening light looking just like someone had thrown handfuls of rainbow hematite into the air. What surprised Lunamor most was that, even though the force of the falling water clearly caused strong vibrations through the ground, the cacophony of noise he would have expected was completely missing. Over the gentle rumble of the river passing by him, Lunamor could just make out a melodic tinkling sound as though the water droplets were made of the most delicate crystals.

Although awestruck by the impressive sight before him, Lunamor had not lost his sense of purpose and had been relieved to see that he finally had an answer to the conundrum of how he was going to cross the river. The Kriolk mountains were at the southernmost boundary of this world and Lunamor had assumed that the river also originated at the very southernmost lip of the land. What he now saw before him showed that he had been very wrong. The jet of water which surged from the mountain to create the river didn't reach land at the boundary of the world but further inland. This meant that Lunamor only needed to continue to follow the river's course. He would eventually reach the point where the water met land and he could travel around the back of the shower of water which fell to the ground at this point. He would then be able to reach the mountains and begin to climb.

Lunamor was well aware that the Toihora could be waiting for him on the other side and he did not particularly want to come face to face with them again, especially at night, so he decided that this would be a good place to sleep for the night. He had plenty of food in his pack, provided by the Amalona, and it was a reasonably warm night so there would be no need to light a fire. Lunamor felt a shiver of excitement as he realised that, by tomorrow, he would be almost at his destination.

Chapter 32

As soon as the first rays of morning light sliced through the darkness of night, Lunamor continued his journey. The steady stream of water falling gracefully from the mountain was as beautiful in the wan dawn light as it had been the evening before.

Lunamor strode out purposefully, noticing that the closer he came to the powerful jet of water the more moisture there was in the air. The force with which the water hit the ground not only caused the constant thrumming vibrations through the ground but also caused a light mist to fill the air. Lunamor imagined this is what it would feel like to walk through a cloud and quite enjoyed the refreshing coolness of the purest of waters on his face.

As he almost came level to the point where the water made contact with the ground though, Lunamor began to shiver uncontrollably. The fine mist that had been almost welcoming before had now drenched Lunamor through to his skin. It was also no longer a fine mist and Lunamor felt as though he was walking through a monsoon rain. The spray from the jet of water bounced off in all directions and Lunamor found himself very disorientated. Blindly, he felt out with each foot, ensuring that there was solid ground beneath his feet. Always in the back of his mind was the thought that if he blundered on without any care he could easily step off the land and into the swiftly flowing waters of the river.

Moonstone, by slow moonstone, Lunamor worked his way round the back of the falling jet of water. It's steady arc towered over his head and standing under the downpour was like standing underneath a transparent glass bridge. Lunamor could just see the blue of the sky beyond the sheet of water over his head albeit slightly blurred.

Transfixed, Lunamor forgot all about how cold and uncomfortable he was and, for just a few minutes, he allowed himself the enjoyment of seeing such a marvellous wonder. If he ever returned to Caamond, this was what he would tell Kuu about. He knew that his Founder would have appreciated the beauty of the river's beginnings. He wouldn't tell of the dangers he had faced, he wouldn't bore Kuu with tales of the nights he had felt so lonely, homesick and lost. He would share with Kuu all the best things he had seen of this world of theirs. And when he had told Kuu, he would tell the rest of the Eternal Children. He would show them that there was more to life than the restrictive confines of the city walls.

Sadly, Lunamor wasn't sure if that day would ever come and for now he needed to focus on the task ahead. Physically shaking himself out of his reverie, he realised that he had become almost entranced by the hypnotic effects of the falling water. It would be so easy to stand here and watch this miracle of nature take place but he knew that staying here would be the death of him. He would eventually freeze to death as the icy waters chilled him through to the bone. This would cause his heart to slow and he would eventually fall into a sleep that he would never wake up from. He wondered how many others might have fallen prey to this spectacle. How many others might have allowed death to take them as they struggled to tear their eyes away from the vision before them?

He knew he needed to move but for some reason his feet refused to obey his will. It was as though the awesome display before him had hypnotised him and he did not have the power to break the spell and yet, in the back of his mind, Lunamor was completely aware of what was happening to him. This made the helplessness even more terrifying. Lunamor was unable to tear his gaze away but, as he stared unblinkingly into the torrent of water, the light began to take on a new quality. It was imperceptible at first but steadily the strength of this new light became stronger and Lunamor found that he was able to sweep his eyes away from the arc of water above him and look down towards where this new source of light was being emitted from. Lunamor's eyes locked onto the crystal which hung around his neck. It was no longer a solid lilac colour but was instead a rainbow of colours which swirled and sparkled from within its smooth surfaces. The light it gave out was becoming brighter and brighter until the captivating brilliance of the bridge of water was no longer any competition for the powerful glow of Lunamor's crystal. Lunamor felt free will return to his body and visibly shook the powerful effects of the river's source from him as easily as he shook the water from his hair.

Lunamor took a tentative step, and then another, feeling his legs tremble with the cold and the after effects of the realisation that he had almost allowed himself to freeze to death under the ice cold waters. Miniature rainbows speckled his skin as the sun's rays bounced off each individual crystal clear drop of water and Lunamor held out his arms in wonder at the beautiful effect this created. The crystal around his neck continued to glow but, as he stepped out from underneath the flow of water and into the bright sunlight of day, the light immediately blinked out. For a moment Lunamor was completely blinded as the crystal's fierce light remained imprinted onto his eyes. As his vision cleared, Lunamor found himself once again standing at the foot of the Kriolk mountains.

Chapter 33

Unlike the last time he had stood before the Kriolk mountains, much further to the west, this time he could see a narrow winding path which led up the steep mountainside. Lunamor allowed his gaze to slowly follow the course of the track until it was swallowed up by the thick haze of fog which seemed to permanently shroud the highest part of the mountain from view. Tendrils of mist curled and unfurled like fingers beckoning him onwards and upwards.

The journey up the mountain was not going to be easy however Lunamor was relieved that he did not have to climb the sheer rock face and he was also reassured that there seemed to be none of the hostile Toihora in sight. With his clothing and hair steaming from the heat of the day, which quickly began to evaporate the water he had been drenched with, Lunamor found the point where the trail started and began his journey upwards. It was almost impossible for him to believe that his voyage might soon be at an end. By nightfall he may finally have found the place he could call home with those who would be his true ancestors. He may even find enlightenment on the subject of the prophecy and discover, once and for all, what danger it spoke of and what it had to do with him.

Lunamor's heart felt light and his step was likewise as he began to make his way along the path. The track wasn't steep but gently inclined upwards, meandering backwards and forwards across the north facing side of the mountain. At times, it became treacherously narrow and Lunamor found himself having to edge around rock falls or shrubbery that blocked the way. As long as he didn't look down, Lunamor found this part of his journey almost enjoyable. The suns had now dried out his clothes and, as he climbed higher and higher, Lunamor was able to look out over the land before him. To the east he could see the boglands of the Amalona and, racing past the boglands, the swift flowing river. Beyond that he could make out a dark green hazy blur which stretched from east to west and which, Lunamor knew, was the forest of Morupo. Lunamor gave a sad smile as he thought of Rendol and wondered what the funny little creature was doing right now. From this vantage point, Lunamor was unable to see the encampment of the Wind Speeder dragons and he gave a silent thanks to them for their part in getting him this far.

Lunamor's trek up the mountain had been surprisingly uneventful so far, in fact it had been thoroughly enjoyable, and Lunamor had settled into an easy, relaxed stride. It was for this reason that he did not worry, at first, about the gentle breeze that had sprung up. It gently tugged at his clothing and blew a few stray strands of hair away from his face. Lunamor welcomed the refreshing coolness of it as his exertions had begun to make him quite hot. It was only when his long grey curls began to sweep across his face, obscuring his vision, that he realised that the wind had become much stronger. Loose stones and vegetation swept past his feet and scuttled over the edge of the trail, rattling away down the cliff face. The strengthening wind caused a fine red dust to rise up into the air and Lunamor had to squint his eyes against the bits of grit which flew into his face.

With the force of the wind buffeting his body, and the dust filled air obscuring his vision, Lunamor realised the perilous position he was in. It would take only one strong gust of wind to suddenly snatch him away from his perch upon the mountain and he would plummet down to the rocky ground below. Lunamor shuffled his feet slowly forward making sure that his back stayed as close to the mountain wall as possible. He reached out with his arms, searching for anything on the smooth rock wall to hold onto. With a sigh of relief, Lunamor was able to grasp the roots of a sinewy tree which grew from the rocky surface. To Lunamor, it seemed as though this action enraged the wind, as though the wind was capable of thought and emotion, and the strength of the wind increased to epic proportions. It tore ferociously at Lunamor's clothing and buffeted his body as though trying to push him over the edge. It howled like a creature possessed and Lunamor was almost certain he heard words hidden within the cacophony of sound: "Jump", "Give up", "Go back", "Die".

"Never!" screamed Lunamor in defiance into the maelstrom of surging wind, dust and debris. As though a switch had been flicked, all suddenly became still. Lunamor was unable to feel even the slightest puff of air. The few wispy clouds in the sky seemed to hang motionless. Every tiny leaf of the numerous plants which dotted the path remained still as though made of stone. The only thing that moved was Lunamor as he sank, with relief, to the ground. His eyes streamed with water as they tried to clear his vision of the dust that had blown into them. Lunamor was overcome with fatigue and the hopeless sense that some invisible force was doing its best to prevent him getting to where he needed to be. A vision of Kuu came to his mind and Lunamor realised that if he ever wanted to see his Founder again he needed to keep moving. He needed to not give up. With this thought in mind Lunamor rose to his feet and continued his journey up the mountainside.

Chapter 34

Lunamor continued to climb steadily higher and higher. The further up the mountainside he progressed, the more of Orokuvar he could see stretching out below him. A world that, until his exile, he had known nothing about. Even at this height Lunamor could not see the city of Caamond nor the northern border of Orokuvar. Having travelled all this distance south he was curious about what lay north of Caamond. If the power of his crystal had not guided him south, would he have maybe travelled northwards instead? What might he have encountered in that direction? Would he have found somewhere to call home in that direction and therefore never have heard about the prophecy or his part in it? Not knowing the nature of the dangers his world faced, Lunamor was unable to comprehend what the consequences might have been had he not been guided by his crystal and the geode he carried.

Without conscious thought, Lunamor had travelled quite a distance up the mountainside and he now noticed that tendrils of fog drifted across the trail in front of him. At this height, the fog was only a light mist and Lunamor was able to still make out the pathway before him as well as the clusters of twisted bushes and plants which protruded directly from the cliff face. But with every step Lunamor took, the fog became denser and denser until he felt as though he was stepping out into an abyss. Lunamor's breath began to come in short sharp bursts as panic began to set in. He couldn't possibly continue climbing up the mountainside when he was unable to see where he placed his feet. He shuffled his feet along the floor and kept his shoulder pressed tight against the rocky wall at his side. At this pace, he would never reach the summit before nightfall and Lunamor knew that, if it was a dangerous path he walked now, it would be treacherous were he to continue onwards through thick fog and the black of night. This gave him no choice but to cautiously continue upwards.

Suddenly, Lunamor lurched forward and he realised that his right foot had shuffled out into nothingness. With nothing to grab onto and with a complete sense of disorientation, Lunamor plunged forward. He gave a scream of alarm and tensed his body in anticipation of the expected plummet to the ground. Oddly, this didn't happen and before Lunamor knew what had happened his fall was over before it had begun. He found himself sprawled on his hands and knees on the trail. Sitting up shakily, Lunamor felt along the ground he had just travelled and was able to make out a hollow in the path he had just been walking. It was into this that he had just fallen. He took an unsteady breath in and then out, then again, giving his trembling body a chance to calm and his heart to stop pounding.

Lunamor climbed unsteadily to his feet and, making sure that the wall was still at his left shoulder, he continued on up the mountain. He was tempted to crawl but, irrationally, the thought of tipping face first over the edge was more terrifying than the thought of stepping out into thin air. Lunamor had lost all sense of time and had no idea how long he stumbled along in the blinding fog. He knew it must still be daytime as there was a white haze to the fog as the sun struggled to force its way through the grey veil which completely obscured the topmost heights of the mountain. Lunamor kept his left hand flat against the wall and brushed his palm along the roughly textured mountainside as he climbed onwards.

All of a sudden, there was nothing but air against Lunamor's fingers. He stopped walking and reached out with his left hand, trying to make contact with the wall's surface again. Still nothing. It was then that Lunamor became aware of a cool breeze coming from where the mountain wall should have been. How was that possible? Surely there should be solid rock there. Lunamor inched further forward and, as he did so, the quality of light began to change. Whereas before, Lunamor could only just see his hand in front of his face; he now could make out dark shapes to either side of him and a strange glow ahead. He stretched his arms out to both sides and realised that he had stepped into an opening in the wall of the mountain. Hesitantly, still unsure of the footing ahead of him, Lunamor moved deeper into the mountain face, leaving the perilous edge behind him. As he continued forward, the fog became thinner and thinner and Lunamor was now able to make out the red walls of rock on either side of him and the long narrow tunnel stretching out before him.

It was impossible to see where the tunnel led and Lunamor had no idea how far the tunnel would take him into the centre of the mountain. What he did know was that, for the moment, he was safer here than he was on the path he had just left behind. He also knew that the tunnel must open out somewhere as he could still see the glow of daylight ahead of him. Moving more quickly now, Lunamor passed along the tunnel, the light at the end becoming brighter and brighter as he moved onwards. He also became aware of a low roar which became louder the closer he moved towards the light. Before he realised it, Lunamor had suddenly stepped out into dazzling sunlight and the most breathtaking sight he had ever seen lay before him.

Chapter 35

Lunamor found himself standing on a precipice on the far side of the mountain he had been steadily climbing up. Plummeting away from the mountain, just beneath the ledge he stood on, was a magnificent waterfall which plunged downwards into a cushion of billowing white clouds. The tremendous noise of the waterfall pounded in his ears but Lunamor hardly noticed so mesmerised was he by the majesty of the spectacle before him.

The suns shone on the mirror-like surface of the waterfall which cascaded flawlessly down the mountainside without even the slightest ripple. Mounds of the purest white cloud spread out before him as though the land were made of this material. The peaks as the hills and the troughs as the valleys with the occasional hollow which seemed to mimic the lakes and the seas of Lunamor's own world. And into this fluffy land sank the waters of the waterfall without ever disturbing the pristine blanket below. In stark contrast to the alabaster blanket was the cyan blue of the sky with nothing to mar its pristine surface; no birds, clouds or even insects to spot the perfect canvas before him.

All at once, Lunamor felt himself being thrown off balance and was only just able to stop himself falling over the edge by throwing his weight backwards towards the tunnel entrance behind him. Lunamor stumbled backwards and found himself sprawled on the uneven surface. Propping himself up on his elbows, he looked around him in panic, looking for whatever it was that had almost knocked him over the edge. It was then that he saw a most impressive sight. Pummelling the air around it, suspended in the bluest of blue skies, was the most exquisitely beautiful dragon Lunamor had ever seen or heard tell of.

The dragon thrashed its wings powerfully and as it did so droplets of water flew off in all directions. To Lunamor, this appeared at first to be because the dragon had flown through the waterfall, but then he realised that the dragon was in fact formed of crystal clear water. As Lunamor watched in awe he realised that he could, in fact, see right through the dragon. The scenery beyond the dragon rippled slightly as the fluid form of the dragon hovered mere moonstones away from where Lunamor stood. Within the dragon's chest Lunamor could just make out, where its heart would be, a perfectly formed pearl which pulsed palely as though with life.

Just then, within his head, Lunamor could hear a tinkling voice which, instinctively, he knew to be the voice of the breathtakingly stunning dragon before him. "I am Perla, the only Amanzi dragon of this world. My purpose is to serve you". With that, Lunamor found himself being swept onto Perla's back by the force of the Amanzi dragon's powerful wings. The dragon's back felt smooth and cool under Lunamor's touch but Lunamor was surprised to find that despite its fluid appearance it was firm and able to hold his weight. Without saying anything further, Perla soared downwards to the thick blanket of cloud below. Just as Lunamor thought they were going to be swallowed by the white haze, Perla skimmed the surface causing little puffs of cloud to fly up in all directions. Lunamor felt his stomach being left behind as they swiftly lifted back up into the sky. Up and up the Amanzi dragon flew. Her smooth stomach remained parallel to the mountainside and Lunamor clung on for dear life, terrified that if he let go he would fall forever.

After only a few minutes of flight, Lunamor could see the summit of the mountain and, before he knew it, the Amanzi dragon had crested the edge of the mountain top and deposited Lunamor on its flat surface. Again, he heard the tinkling voice in his head, like shards of crystal clinking together, "I am yours to command, as and when you need me. You need only call my name and I will come no matter where you be". And with that, Perla, the Amanzi dragon, lifted back up into the air and then dropped back over the mountain side and out of sight.

Still breathless from his flight up the mountainside, Lunamor turned away from the mountain edge to face what awaited him.

Chapter 36

Looking around him, Lunamor noticed that the top of the mountain was completely flat. He also noticed that he was not alone. There, in front of him, was some kind of settlement. It consisted of a number of wooden shelters of a type he hadn't seen before. The wood they were made of was highly polished and of a dark ebony colour. They had small chimneys from which puffed small clouds of grey smoke. All of the huts had windows of glass but each of the windows was unique in that they were made of stained glass and each depicted a coat of arms. Lunamor assumed that these represented the families that resided within.

Most of the doors of the huts stood open and Lunamor saw that there were families gathered at the threshold of the homes watching him reverently. They gazed steadily at him, neither afraid nor surprised to see him. Strangely, Lunamor felt no fear either despite the fact that his journey so far had been full of peril and despite the fact that he had met as many enemies as he had friends. Soundlessly, one figure moved forward from amongst the rest, stopping only when he was face to face with Lunamor.

The figure before him was so alike in appearance to himself, that Lunamor felt as though he could have been looking in a mirror. The figure was tall and muscular with the same curly grey hair. His smile was warm and, as he reached out to grasp Lunamor's hands in welcome, Lunamor noticed that this stranger, who did not feel like a stranger, bore the same strange symbol on his neck. A feeling of finally being with family overwhelmed Lunamor as he was pulled into a friendly embrace, "Welcome home," the stranger whispered softly into his ear.

As the figure pulled away he introduced himself, "I'm Maran, spokesperson for the Eternal Keepers. We have waited a long time for you". Maran led Lunamor over to a massive hut which had been hidden by the smaller huts in front of it. He guided Lunamor through the huge double doors and Lunamor found himself in some kind of meeting hall. At one end, stood a lectern and fanned out from this, in a huge semi-circle, were rows and rows of benches. Many of the benches at the front were filled with more figures who looked just like Lunamor and, as Lunamor and Maran entered the building, those Eternal Keepers who had stood at their own doors followed and took a seat upon the benches until the hall was full and only standing room remained at the back.

Lunamor followed Maran until they both stood, side by side, behind the lectern. Maran then motioned for all those gathered to settle down before he began to speak. "The Exiled Child we have heard tell of, from the prophecy and from our folklore stands here now before us. He has many things he needs to learn and we may be impatient for action but we must wait. Only part of the prophecy has yet come to bear and that is that the Exiled Child exists but his very presence here and now only tells us that the evils foretold follow not far behind". As the Eternal Keeper spoke these solemn words, looks of fear were exchanged between the inhabitants of this mountaintop settlement. Without any further words, Maran dismissed the rapt crowd and slowly they began to disperse, throwing the occasional curious look over their shoulders as they went.

Once they were alone, Maran turned to face Lunamor, "You need to eat and rest. Shortly before sundown, I will come to you and we will talk". Lunamor was so overcome with emotion he was unable to speak. A kaleidoscope of emotions twirled within him; confusion, grief, fear, love and other emotions he couldn't define. He felt as though he had lost so much on his journey to this point but he had also gained something significant at the same time. Maran hadn't said so but Lunamor knew these people were his ancestors. He had many questions he needed answers to but he knew that, in time, these answers would come.

Lunamor allowed himself to be taken to an empty hut where food had been laid out on a small square table with a clean silvery cloth laid over it. Upon the table were heaped plates of food and a jug of fresh water. Maran patted Lunamor gently on the back and then left him in peace. It felt like a lifetime ago since Lunamor had last eaten and he ate until he thought he would never want to eat again. He emptied the jug of water, glad to clear his throat and mouth of the dust that had gathered on his travels up the mountainside. Appetite and thirst sated, Lunamor then rose from the table and pulled aside a clean white sheet which was draped across a doorway beyond which he found a small but comfortable looking bed. Lunamor was just able to find the energy to remove his boots, lay the geode and the palisade he carried under the feather pillow and lay his head down before he drifted away into a deep slumber.

Chapter 37

It seemed that Lunamor had only just closed his eyes, when he felt himself being gently shook awake. Blearily, he prised his eyelids open to see the elected leader of the Eternal Keepers standing over him. Lunamor came awake instantly, keen to hear what Maran had to tell him. The light in the room had subtly changed and Lunamor could tell that night was slowly approaching. "Come," gestured Maran with a casual jerk of his shoulder, "We will talk outside".

Lunamor rose from the bed, shoved his feet into his shoes and followed Maran out of the hut and into the dying rays of the suns. Lunamor found Maran waiting just outside the hut. He was sitting on a fallen log which was being used as a bench. Quietly, he took a seat beside the Eternal Keeper. Without hesitation, Maran began to speak. "I know you have many, many questions you will wish to ask some of which I have answers to and some of which you will need to discover for yourself. Let me start by telling you a little bit about our people, about your people to be more precise". At these words, Lunamor felt relief flood his body. He had felt as though he belonged here but hearing Maran confirm this put any doubts he may have had from his mind.

"We are the Eternal Keepers. Our role is to act as guardians of this world. You are one of us but you are so much more. You have many names; the prophet refers to you as Crystal Bearer and Exiled Child, the citizens of Caamond knew you as an Eternal Child and we recognise you as one of our own, a true Eternal Keeper. It is for this reason that our ancestors went in search of you many years ago, hoping to bring you home with them and prepare you for the challenges that lay ahead of you. Fate had different plans, however, and it seems now as though this journey you have undertaken was vital in order for you to appreciate the beauty of Orokuvar and to respect it at the same time."

"But what challenges lay ahead, and why me?" blurted Lunamor. Maran tilted his head to one side as though considering the questions Lunamor had asked. "The question of, why you, is not a question the likes of you or I can answer. It is a greater being than us that decides the fates of this world and its inhabitants. As for the question of what dangers we face, I fear that whatever this evil is it is worse than anything we could imagine. I feel that we still have some time left to prepare but not long. And now, I have something I would like to show you".

Maran rose from the log and began to walk away. Lunamor wanted to protest, to demand that Maran clarify what he meant by having time to prepare. How could Maran possibly know how long they had left? How could Maran know what preparations they needed to make? Instead, he dutifully followed close behind. The Eternal Keeper approached the northern edge of the mountain top and stood facing out over Orokuvar. With one hand he gestured Lunamor forward and then stepped away and behind so that Lunamor could behold the sight before him.

There in front of him lay the whole of his world. From his vantage point upon the highest pinnacle of Orokuvar, Lunamor saw three spheres hanging in the sky in front of him; the two suns with the silver moon in the centre. Directly underneath the three spheres lay the city of Caamond, its borders laid out in the familiar star shape

Lunamor had lived confined within for most of his young life. Surrounding everything, Lunamor could see nine of the straight edges which made up the hendecagon shaped world Lunamor lived in with the tenth edge being the one on which the Kriolk mountains stood.

Almost absent-mindedly, Lunamor fingered the symbol on his neck and it was only now he was able to see what it represented. The symbol was a representation of the world of Orokuvar. It showed that he belonged to the world and the world belonged to him. He knew then that, whatever dangers he might face, whatever evils he had to fight, this was his fate. He could not escape his destiny and, whatsmore, he didn't want to. Since leaving the safety and security of the city walls of Caamond, he had faced many dangers and had feared for his life at times. For the first time since hearing of the prophecy, Lunamor finally believed that he was the one it spoke of.

With a new determination in his heart, Lunamor looked out over his world, Orokuvar, and a small smile flickered across his face as he watched the two suns sink below the lip of the world, one after the other, and the silvery sheen of the moon spread its magic light across the land. How fitting that he should finally arrive home on the eve of the Silver Eclipse.

Printed in Great Britain
by Amazon